Growing up in Sydney

Growing up in Sydney

Daniel Lo Surdo

for the village that has supported me

An Ode to Home – Submission to the Clarendon Chronicle (R. Leonardi – Year 12)

You don't have to read Dickens to know the tale of two cities. If you're in Sydney, you can see both from your bedroom window.

Sailboats gliding past the Opera House and Harbour Bridge are a picture of grace and serenity. The kind only found on an island-continent blessed with self-complimentary ideals of Medicare and gun control.

I get sad when imagining what a tourist would think of Sydney. The feeling on the ground is much less peaceful than the pictures on the postcards. The city is dirty, buildings awkward, and people hardly pleasant. And that's just around The Rocks.

The brochures don't show the undercurrent swirling beneath the champagne sailors and catamarans. The counterswell slapping up against the bling. The people scanning the tickets and pouring the grog. Flogging fake boomerangs next to the Manly ferry.

Sydneysiders are in one of two tribes. They're either serving canapes, or politely declining them. The latte line is too frothy to stand on.

It leaves me feeling melancholy. You're nothing more than your job and postcode, the place you study, or the car you drive.

No upswell of empathy or understanding will change that. Not in Sydney.

1

Raffaele 'Rusty' Leonardi

September 2022

Vuup. Turn. Bang. My head smacks the thinly carpeted floor, leaving a nasty burn up the length of my cheek. Panicking, I spring up and swivel to face the muffled sounds descending the corridor.

I soon realise what it is, and the panic goes away. I can hear Patrick, James, and Jack chuckling at the end of the corridor. I check my phone—3:47. They must be on their way home. One last prank. I pick my mattress up, throw it back on its frame, and go to bed. I don't give them the satisfaction, not that they'd still be watching me anyway. I throw the sheet over my body, and face towards my window. *Best room in the dorm Rusty!*, my Housemaster told me. *Besides the seniors.*

But I wasn't so sure. It made me a prime candidate for a mattress-flipping; furthest away from the teachers' rooms and at the end of the student corridor. It provided my classmates the perfect escape back to their own rooms, leaving enough time to be back in bed before a teacher could catch them, but short enough to not wake their victim.

My window overlooked the main quadrangle, where most of the day students would meet before class. I looked out each morning to see if there was anyone worth seeing. Otherwise, I'd sit by my desk, finishing off homework or doing some last-minute cramming before an exam.

Some of the country boarders used my room on the weekends to smoke weed. My window gave them a perfect view to patrol for teachers. *The best room in the dorm.* They would leave the window ajar, presumably to get the smell out. I would shut it every Friday, to stop the rain from falling onto my windowsill. The swirling wind was always a danger on the top of the school hill.

Another time, I found a butt resting between two bricks outside my window. I pinched it from the mortar, hid it in my fist, and, when the coast was clear, tucked it under Patrick's pillow. That was a few months ago. I haven't had a problem since.

I had been flipped before. An initiation was inevitable. Except it didn't come in my first week. It was on a Friday night at the start of winter, when I stayed in the House ahead of my rugby match on Saturday.

To keep you from the outside noise Rusty, my Housemaster told me. While the teachers were getting drunk in the quadrangle, five boys – all on my floor – snuck through the corridor, crept their hands over my body, and spun my mattress to the floor.

One of the sports coaches must have heard the bang, the roar of laughter, or a combination of both. He snapped from his evening buzz and stormed into the House, giving them all a real scolding. He and I shared a smile when we beat Saint Marys the next afternoon. I gave the same look to the boys in the grandstand after the game, but they ignored my gaze.

Tonight was the first time I'd been flipped since then. Yesterday was the second last day of the term, and the last for the country boarders before they left for holidays. The school didn't want to punish them for living so far away, so they gave them the last day to travel back to their families, most of which either made their money on farms or in mines. And prayed their sons wouldn't have to do the same.

Because it was their last day, it meant some of the teachers were also packing up for the term. Those who didn't spend their night preparing for two weeks of couch-surfing were at the pub down the road, doing the things they'd spent the last six hours telling their students not to do. They always had a parent or sibling happy to take them in. It was all very carefree.

Patrick, James, and Jack had returned to their beds or the bus, and silence had returned to the halls of Fairfax House. I couldn't get back to sleep. My head was ringing from smashing into the carpet – just a thin veil protecting the wooden floorboards underneath – and my cheek was too tender to set down on the pillow.

I sat up, threw my sports jacket on, and went for a walk. It was the third week of spring, but it still felt like winter. This was especially so at school, where it could freeze on the big hill overlooking the rest of suburbia.

From one spot in the science labs, you could see the Parramatta River and each of Sydney's city centres in the one picture. It suggested there was a world beyond the castle gates.

I didn't want to be in the boarding house any longer. I inched my thongs down the four flights of stairs, past all the juniors, and, silently, through the front door. It was best not to cause a stir. A combination of neurosis and cynicism among teachers made everyone a target. Good faith didn't exist.

I pulled the door 20 centimetres and slipped through. I had taken my thongs off my feet and had hooked them around my index finger. I kept them off until I reached the grass leading to the chapel, which led to the humanities wing and the locker rooms for the day boys.

Until, finally, the science labs. They were on the fifth level of the main building, on top of the classrooms used for the odd sod subjects. Agriculture, graphics, technology, and visual arts. The ones Clarendon didn't care about.

The janitor usually locked the steps to the labs, though he must've forgotten tonight. I took two stairs with every step until I reached level five. The wind was even stronger here. I could feel raindrops on my head. I walked past the two main labs and perched myself on the corner of the building. My legs swung from the balcony, back and forth, the road out of school fifty metres beneath them. I was immeasurable, if but for a millisecond.

2

Clarendon, Phil, and Rusty's Mum

September 2022

I hadn't always been protected, let alone respected, at school. That all started this year. I came back six inches taller than I was in Year 9, with a bit of bicep definition. During the second week back, I was taken out of class by Mr Branderson, a burly, tanned surfer dude with an obsession for young boys who could run quickly with a ball.

I hadn't cared too much for sport before that. A necessity before I could enjoy the weekend, I relegated myself to the bottom teams so I could play early on Saturday and stay off campus until Sunday evening. That wasn't to say I wasn't good. I'd temper my ability, scoring a few tries here and there, but nothing to arouse suspicion from some of the overly serious coaches. That now seemed to be over.

Branderson put a six-month gym schedule in my hand. He had been speaking with my Housemaster, who agreed to supervise and sign off on each of my workouts. *In for a big year*, Branderson assured me. And just like that, I was in the in-crowd. I was being peddled to the front of the dining hall queue and given my Clarendon rugby two-litre stainless steel water bottle. These were the only ones that were allowed into the classroom. Except for the ones with 'Clarendon rowing' on them.

School became an engulfing routine. Workouts on either side of the day's lessons, plus a full Saturday schedule. I eventually convinced Branderson to let me go home on Friday nights, but only with the agreement that Phil – my stepdad – would drive me back for breakfast in the dining hall. None of the other boys had special arrangements in place. I guess I was the lucky one.

The pomp of the rugby school arena was truly a sight to behold. Generic chanting, diplomacy, exclusion, RM Williams boots, $5 sausage sizzles. The religion of 3pm on Saturday felt akin to 9am on Sunday.

I became Clarendon-famous on the Monday morning after the Saturday afternoon. Heads turned at the Year 10 wog kid running down the wing. I liked it at first. The things that used to be said to hurt me was now being used for endearment. I got invited to parties. The Year 12s bought beers for me.

Even the headmaster knew my name. He tried to pronounce the full Raffaele Leonardi at first, but I assured him that Rusty was just fine.

The adoration would pass by Tuesday, and I'd be back to normal without many distractions. The new normal, that is, the one with no waits for meals, and an automatic excuse to replace my bottle of water. It was only really Branderson and Housemaster Patterson, the short, childless man in his late fifties who'd been at Clarendon for over 30 years, who saw me as something worth preserving. The novelty of the Saturday religion soon wore off on my classmates too. But there were fewer jokes at my expense, and some newfound respect.

I enjoyed playing first grade. I didn't like waiting around for 3 o'clock, and the politics that came with it, but the on-field action was a lot of fun.

It was the fruits of my amateurish labour that I loathed. Passing around drinks and girls with the rest of the team on Saturday nights, and the hours-long retelling of war stories from earlier that day. I'd usually duck back to the dorm after the game, grab my textbooks to use the next day, and try to avoid any school-related talk until Monday morning. Even when I got back to the House on Sunday, it'd be after dinner and once everyone was back to their dorms. Or after they had snuck out of them.

For the first time, Mum started coming to my games. Next to Phil, of course. She never had any common ground with the other parents. The ones who holidayed together, had their tee-time every week, and, in all likelihood, played on this very ground, for this very school, 30 years ago.

Phil didn't go to Clarendon, but a carbon-copy school just down the road. If the school's admiration grew for me after I started playing first grade, Phil's had skyrocketed. He started stocking the pantry with Powerades and protein powders within an hour of seeing my gym schedule, which had been tucked between textbooks and stationery scattered across the kitchen table one weekend earlier in the year.

One Friday in term one, I came home to a fully decked-out home gym, in the driveway where his BMW used to live. Resting by the wooden fence was a pull-up stand, with some free weights and an adjustable weight bench sitting at a 90-degree angle. Waiting for me to wear in. I felt a bit embarrassed, considering I was only here on the weekends. How he could reach me, he must've thought. Mum told me to be grateful, and I was. I broke it in the next morning and would always make an effort if I saw Phil sitting in view of the driveway.

He came to each game in the Clarendon rugby polo shirt Branderson gave me when I started my program. And a matching cap he bought from the uniform shop. Every game, just before kick-off, he would walk to the top of the grandstand, Mum trailing behind, and shake all the important hands with a beaming smile on his face. Branderson would kill me if he saw me staring at the grandstand so close to kick-off. He was too busy working with the forwards to notice.

***

I was 11 when I first met Phil. The idea of a boyfriend, let alone a step-dad, was never brought up with me before. So, seeing one at the end of our townhouse was bizarre. And a shock for some time.

He was a short man with red hair. Cleanly shaven, pale skin, blue eyes, and pencil-thin lips. He wore his navy-blue Sydney 2000 Olympics sports coat like a limb, usually over a loose-fitting striped or patterned button-up.

He was introduced as a friend, but this wasn't fooling anyone. Even the gullible child he loomed in front of. He walked four paces towards me, knelt on one knee, offered his forearm and made a fist. I raised my arm and bumped my fist against his. Phil and Mum expelled a wave of nervous laughter and walked into the kitchen to open a bottle of wine. I shuffled back to my room for a lie-down.

Mum was pensive; she always looked pensive, but it was just so overly pronounced this time. She didn't say anything after Phil left, only smiling at the floor briefly before rushing back to the kitchen to fetch me a bowl of ice cream. I didn't say anything; I didn't want to push her into any corners, and felt that an explanation would be forthcoming anyway.

Phil started coming over more and more that year. He even started picking me up from school some days. *Doing your Mum a favour*, he told me. He drove a sandy-brown BMW Sedan, that looked like it was from the nineties. It was the most interesting colour in the pick-up lane that day, sparkling amongst the oyster grey and black shadow covering the rest of the road.

The only trouble was that Phil's car wasn't registered by the school as a parent or guardian's car. It certainly couldn't pass as Mum's ugly silver Renault, and the overly serious teacher – with her clipboard and whistle in hand – stung him straight away. Phil ended up having to get Mum on the phone to explain the situation. She was closing the books for a client during an urgent liquidation, she told the teacher on duty, so she got her partner to pick me up from school. That whole sentence was news to me.

The teacher pinched the smirk on the ends of her lips and relented. She added Phil's car make, registration, and model to her clipboard, and let me go home. We didn't talk much on the drive back. Phil was a freelance consultant (whatever that meant), so he could work his own hours (however that worked).

He pulled into my driveway and walked me to the front door. He scoured the keychain on his belt loop, but I stopped him before he could find the house keys. I didn't know why Mum had given him a key.

I fished out the spare key from under the doormat after five seconds of searching, then twisted the latch. I thanked him for the lift and walked in. Phil was at home when I got back from school the next day. *For dinner*, Mum said. *A thank you for picking you up.*

He moved in the following year. Mum told me he still had an apartment somewhere in the city, but that he didn't have much use for it anymore and was going to rent it out to other people.

The plan was always to go to St Ives High. To stay with my friends. It wasn't like I had other options, but I never wanted to go to another school anyway. It was close to the park where we played footy on Fridays, and pretty much the whole year group ended up going there. It was just the done thing.

Phil, who seemed to be doing much more personal consulting than for work, offered an alternative. *Clarendon College*. The name didn't ring a bell. *The castle near the water?* Mum asked. Phil nodded his head. His old teacher from school, who he was now mates with, taught ancient history there, and reckoned he could push me up the waitlist.

What's the harm? Mum asked. I shrugged my shoulders. Mum assured me that the plan was still for me to stay in St Ives with my friends. *But what's the harm in trying, hey Rusty?*

I was fitted for my school blazer six months later. I had to do an entrance exam, but that was easier than the weekly quizzes I'd do at school. I was in. Not just in Year 7, but as a boarder. Phil was a boarder too, back in his day, and said he loved it.

I wasn't sure what it was at first, but I quickly learned I detested it.

Why would I want to stay at school a minute after 3:00? Let alone live there? But it was all too late.

Such an awesome opportunity! Mum was on board. I think this was her way of apologising for me being an only child. Not that I ever complained of a lack of company or being alone. I was happy with my life in St Ives; walking to school, playing soccer during recess and lunchtime, and then kicking the footy after school. I'd play until it was dark, or until Mum pulled me away from the oval.

Phil had started meeting me at the oval after school. He had joined in once, but had dislocated his finger when he'd tried to mark one of my kicks. He brought oranges after that.

We were all just killing time. Some had brothers or sisters at far-away high schools or music rehearsals, or had parents who couldn't leave work before five.

Others would duck home after the final bell, drop off their bags, and greet us with a Sherrin kicked on top of our heads. None had their parents, let alone a de-facto stepdad, join in. It was weird seeing Phil trying to winch the ball off a bunch of 12-year-olds, who could all run circles around him. I think I appreciated his effort.

Mum had stopped coming to pick me up, so I'd just go home with Phil. These afternoons were never meant to change. It would be the same the next year, just in a St Ives High uniform.

***

I signed up for the AFL team on my first day at Clarendon. I even tried my hand at rowing, but that didn't pan out. *Too small*, one of the coaches said when I fronted the trials. I didn't want to lift weights up and down anyway. The footy team folded in Year 8, once the 'gayFL' tag – a homophobic spin on the name for Aussie rules – started being kicked across the schoolyard.

It forced me into the *real* footy (rugby union, that is). First thing Saturday, back in St Ives by lunchtime. I didn't see many of my friends from primary school anymore. It was so much harder without standing plans every afternoon. Simply allowing these friendships to collapse was easier than managing them. We never had to do that back then.

***

Phil and Mum would only visit me at Clarendon for parent-teacher nights. They ended up marrying when I was in Year 9 – last year – a few years after Phil moved in. A big ceremony at a tiny chapel in The Rocks.

I first noticed a big diamond on Mum's ring finger a year before the wedding. I was in the back of the car, the middle seat, when the diamond resting on the side of the console smacked me in the face. I remember Mum's smile. A tiny grin creased at the side of her mouth, and she looked down at the floor, then Phil, in a flux of joy, anxiety, and overwhelm. Phil, trying to focus on the road, smirked at Mum.

Are you gonna tell him?. Mum took a beat, then told me what I had already knew. She screamed in excitement. I made a smile and hugged her over the seat. *I popped the question a couple of weeks ago,* Phil said through his own grin. They had dinner by the Opera House, and he proposed near Mrs Macquarie's Chair, when they were walking back towards the car.

Very postcard, I thought. *Very Sydney.*

They were waiting for the right time to tell me. The three of us had had fish and chips to celebrate. I was happy for Mum. She certainly looked happy. Phil did too. He was freaking out over all the wedding planning too. *A real groomzilla*, Mum was calling him. Three different hardback binders, she told me; one for the service, the other for the reception. Then one for the honeymoon. Mum reluctantly joined in with my laughs.

Phil was going to sell his apartment in the city to fund a renovation of the house. They wanted to convert the attic into a room for me to use on the weekends and were thinking about installing a plunge pool in the backyard. *Mona Vale is too far for a dip*, Phil reasoned.

Mum sheepishly excused herself after we were done with dinner. She wanted to see what the fishermen at the end of the wharf had been able to pull in. It was just Phil and me. He asked me if I was okay with Mum getting remarried, as if I had a say.

Yes, yes of course. Rinse and repeat, until he would stop with his questioning. He then asked if I would be one of his groomsmen. I gave him the same response.

3

Vincenzo Leonardi

June 1970

Vincenzo Leonardi was born on 21 June 1970 in Camperdown, Sydney. The second child of Alessandro and Vittoria, two beneficiaries of a relaxed White Australia policy. They came from a small village in Sicily that, like many others across Italy, had been destroyed in World War Two. The war denied them any opportunity or education. They settled for what they had.

Alessandro spent most of his time on the Mediterranean, throwing out fishing nets and praying he would catch something. Vittoria found work with her neighbour, an elderly lady who had been cleaning the holiday homes of Italy's wealthiest families since the start of the century. If these families had fallen on tough times after the war, they didn't spend like it. She would tend to the houses – completing the washing, cleaning, and dusting – when the families were away, and would cook for their dinner parties when they were holidaying in Sicily.

Alessandro and Vittoria were both making just enough to get by. Their parents had become weak in older age, and couldn't work as much as they once could. This was as good as it would be for them.

They were married shortly after the war. A no-frills formality approved by their respective parents, who were always fond of each other. Alessandro continued to fish, and Vittoria continued to clean. They couldn't afford children. It was difficult to live on their own wages at that point, so adding a child and removing Vittoria's income felt suicidal.

Leaving Sicily was never the plan. They wanted to raise kids on the Mediterranean, enjoying the childhood they were denied. Alessandro was piecing together enough money to buy his own boat, which he could throw a fish net out of each morning. He thought he could make triple the money selling by himself at the fish markets, rather than doing all the work for someone else.

Mussolini's reign was over in Italy, but its effects weren't. Dreams of his own business and a family were fleeting for Alessandro, as making enough to survive became its own challenge. His parents had become unable to work, and Vittoria's income was dwindling as the wealthy families ran out of money.

Alessandro and Vittoria nervously boarded the SS Galileo Galilei in Messina, and arrived in Sydney on 11 June 1964. Their ticket to a better life. Sicilians had been trickling into Australia for about 20 years before they docked in Walsh Bay. Many had since returned to the village to see family, and had spoken positively about life in Australia. Alessandro was always sceptical but knew they must've had some money if they could travel back to Sicily.

They settled in Leichhardt, which had become the undisputed hub for Italians in Sydney by the sixties. It was surprisingly familiar to them. Alessandro knew some fishermen who had moved to Australia in the years after the war, while Vittoria recognised some of the grocers with businesses in Leichhardt. They even spotted Carlo, a Sicilian man who came over shortly after the war. With some money put away, he opened a booming restaurant on Norton Street called *Bar Italia*. It was a place for men to drink, but also catered to families in the area.

Alessandro and Vittoria lived with Matteo Bellomo, a friend of Alessandro's from Sicily. He came to Sydney by himself in 1954 and, much to the ire of his family, married an Australian woman shortly after. Jane, a trainee bank teller who was the daughter of a dock worker and homemaker from Balmain. They bought a three-bedroom – four at a pinch – detached house for a few thousand bucks in 1966, but didn't need much of its space. Jane had given birth to a boy – Giuseppe – one year before Alessandro and Vittoria came to Australia.

Vincenzo – born in 1970 – never met Matteo, Jane, or Giuseppe. Matteo sold the house to Alessandro in 1968. He had been saving every cent from his work by the water since he had arrived in Sydney. Liquidating the house was a term of Matteo and Jane's divorce, which also gave full custody of Giuseppe to his mother. Alessandro and Vittoria heard Matteo went back to Sicily. They never saw him again.

Vittoria was pregnant when Alessandro bought the house. She gave birth to their first child on 18 September 1968. Also called Alessandro, as was the custom for the first-born in the Leonardi family. He was given the middle name of Giovanni – the only name he'd ever been called.

Giovanni and Vincenzo, their second child, were walked to school each day by their mother, who hadn't needed to work since leaving Sicily. She would spend her mornings taking down washing and ironing her boys' uniform – an orange polo with blue shorts – before preparing breakfast and dressing them for school. Alessandro left for work hours before, and would often go days without seeing his children. Vittoria would clean the house, shop for tomatoes and onions at the grocers, and prepare pasta sauce for dinner.

Vincenzo was a short boy with disorderly hair and a crooked smile. At the stern order of his parents, he worked hard at school but was never able to keep up with his classmates. He would be bullied by the other children in his class. He was called names or teased about his packed lunch each day. Focaccia, or a panini with melted cheese and leg ham.

He tried his best until he was 16, when his teachers suggested that continuing at school wasn't his best option. Alessandro and Vittoria cursed their advice, but didn't protest it. They had gone through a similar experience with Giovanni two years earlier.

Vincenzo started work with his father and brother the summer he left school. He started different labouring jobs as he got older, eventually finding some luck with Giovanni on construction sites across the Inner West. The pair gained a reputation as two no-nonsense workers ready to step in during a safety pause or worker strike.

They learned to nurture relationships with government and big property representatives, which helped them negotiate enviable terms when they were desperately needed on a jobsite. The money allowed Alessandro to pull back from his own work on the docks, an overdue order for a weakening man.

4

The Wedding

September 2022

I'd never been to a wedding before. Mum and Phil's was pompous, a bit unpolished, and lots of fun.

The boarding house couldn't really wrap their heads around the whole concept that Mum: a) wasn't already married b) was getting married after already giving birth, and c) wasn't getting married to my dad.

All the usual protocols still had to be followed. I handed in my weekend leave slip on Wednesday morning (the day they were due), got it approved by Patterson on Thursday (the day notice was due), and left the gates on Friday afternoon (the day normal people do it).

Phil rented a big Victorian terrace in the uppity part of the Balmain for the groomsmen the night before the wedding. It took me two buses, and a walk by the harbour foreshore to get there. Mum wasn't allowed to drive me. *Needs to be a secret*, Phil told me. Sure.

The other groomsmen were already there when I arrived. Next to Phil would be the four of us. Phil's two best friends, Simon and John, who he'd met at high school. The two of them would smirk at clever jokes and lambast each other's choice of wine. They worked the same corporate jobs. Neither of them was married, or seemed to have had a serious partner before. Different versions of the same person, I thought.

Phil would be brought in to help with some of their projects. They joked too many times that it was their money paying for the wedding. I could tell Phil didn't like it, but he tried not to show it.

Beside Simon and John was Barry, Phil's impossibly Irish father. He spoke with every bit of an accent, making him almost impossible to understand at times. He and Phil shared the same pale complexion, but Barry kept the Irish attitude and permanent sunburn. He had only been in Australia for the last 50 years.

At the end of the oddball conga line would be me, the teenager who was only there under the arbitrary rules of family.

The night before was tiring, onerous, and a bit stressful. The stylists came over at 8:30pm, bringing with them at least four clotheslines fitted with the official penguin suits for the next day.

I changed straight from my school suit to my wedding tux. It fit me fine, just as it did two weeks ago. The boutonnieres were kept on the kitchen counter, as were the cufflinks and pocket squares. The suits were understated but classy, which seemed the right tone for a wedding of two people in their forties. A midnight black jacket was worn over a simple white shirt with black buttons and a grey tie. The cufflinks were in the colours of Cassius College. Phil, Simon and John were gifted their pair when they graduated over 20 years ago. Pairs were bought for Barry and me.

The next day was nice. Breaking all the house rules, I called Mum when I woke up. She sounded excited, and told me she was looking forward to seeing me as a groomsman. Phil was also excited, I told her, and reassured her that we would confiscate the binders so he could enjoy the day. We both let out a giggle and basked in a moment of calm.

The stylists were back in the house when I walked in the kitchen. As if they never left. Work was being done for Barry, who wanted his suit to be a little less tight. The boutonnieres were now in a special felt box, which we were under strict instruction not to touch. I walked back to my room and waited to be called down.

Barry and I led the convoy of cars from the house to the chapel. Simon, John, and Phil were in the matching black sedan behind us. Phil seemed nervous, but had been showing a relaxed face.

Barry was over the scheduling by the time we got in the car. We didn't say much on the way there. He tried to loosen his collar without moving the tie that had been perfectly placed on his top button, and gave up with an audible huff on the third time of trying. *Fuck's sake*, he whispered under his breath. He fell back into his seat and faced towards the window, like a child on the comedown of a temper tantrum.

We assumed our positions next to Phil, who arrived two minutes after Barry and me. Once settled in, Mum, with her hands clasping a bouquet of flowers, walked down the aisle, to meet us, Phil, and her bridesmaid (Donna, a friend who I'd only met a few times), at the altar. They were married fifteen minutes later.

I was driven to the reception with Barry. It was just down the road, but Phil insisted we all take the cars. *Make it look a bit more smart*, he said. Waiting for us was everyone else at the service. They had walked down in much quicker time.

We were served a three-course lunch while the speeches drew on. I didn't want to make a speech, so I sat at the end of the head table, and took in what everyone else had to say. The room was too impersonal to say anything intimate.

I tried to enjoy the formalities. I did my best to swat away questions from nosy divorcées and housewives about when I would be married, and what I was doing with my life. The dance floor was the easiest place to avoid conversation, though this just put me at centre stage to embarrass myself. Especially when Mum and I were pressured into an impromptu dance routine when the DJ started mixing a slew of Abba songs.

Mum and Phil stayed at the hotel above the reception that night. I gave them both a hug once the music stopped, and kissed Mum on the cheek. I trod towards the Quay in search of a way back to my dorm.

5

Fiona Wallace

February 1979

Fiona Wallace never dreamed of being a wife. She was born in Camperdown in 1979, nine years after her first husband Vincenzo, and a decade after her sister Tammy, who suddenly passed away at the age of 10 months. She died around the same time that Vincenzo was born.

Fiona didn't like to think about Tammy, the sister she never met. She only told her son Rusty about her once, passing on each excruciating detail in the hope that he'd never want to ask her again.

Fiona's parents refused to forget about Tammy. They were both from working-class Scottish families, who came to Sydney in the late sixties looking for work and sunny weather. There was also an appeal in raising children in Australia, where they could spend their weekends on a hiking trail or by the beach, rather than rubbing their hands over a fireplace in Glasgow.

Caroline, Fiona's mother, fell pregnant shortly after arriving in Sydney. Everything was going to plan. They were getting by on the money her husband Jack was bringing in from the shipping yards at Pyrmont, which were desperate for any English-speaking labourers. They had settled in a snug worker's cottage in Marrickville. It was small, but big enough to raise children in. Certainly better than what they'd get back home.

***

Jack and Caroline punished themselves for Tammy's unexplainable death. Jack threw himself into work, while Caroline – who used to help her sister at a preschool back in Glasgow – found a job as a teacher's aide at a nearby school. Their marriage had disintegrated, but divorce was never a viable option. They didn't know why something so joyful had to be snatched away from them.

Caroline's second pregnancy was considered an act of God. She and Jack, bolted together by grief, had scarcely been intimate in the years leading up to Fiona's birth. Their second-born represented a new chance for them, both as parents and in their marriage.

They had settled on naming their new daughter Grace – an undeserved gift. They pivoted upon meeting their child, birthed in a relatively smooth procedure, who had the fairest complexion of skin Jack or Caroline had seen. Fiona it was.

They put all their eggs in Fiona's basket. Caroline never returned to her teaching job, planning instead to become her daughter's full-time tutor from preschool until she was a university graduate. Jack would work overtime most days at the docks, often going days without seeing his daughter. Together, they were hoping to raise a person who wouldn't only succeed for herself, but also for Tammy.

***

Fiona didn't regret her first marriage. Without it, she wouldn't have Rusty. She became a mother on a spring morning in 2006; she was 27 at the time. He brought new meaning to her life. There was now another person who she would be living for.

Marriage to Vincenzo – the son of two very traditional, working-class Italian parents – was never going to be simple. Masquerading as an obliging Sicilian housewife was exhausting; if she was being honest with herself, she knew it would never last for too long. She thought her parents, who she lost contact with after marrying Vincenzo, would be disgusted with the life she had chosen.

Still, Fiona found enough time to be a housewife and a mother, and for her career. But in the end, it was just doomed to fail. Her and Vincenzo's lives were always on different tracks, and her train was leaving the station.

***

Fiona never planned on remarrying. She saw some people after Vincenzo, even going for short romantic getaways in Byron Bay and Noosa. But she would always keep this from Rusty, who she'd drop to his father on her way to the airport. She was determined to be Rusty's mother before she was anything else.

Phil caught her by surprise. He was a soft-spoken, shy man who Fiona met on a work call. He sounded devoid of professional conviction, an impression his erroneous tax advice confirmed.

Phil insisted he buy Fiona a drink the day she cleaned up his mess for him. To Fiona's surprise, Phil was charming; he made self-deprecating jokes about his deficiencies as a tax consultant and, unlike most men she had encountered since leaving Vincenzo, seemed to take a genuine interest in her life. They started meeting more regularly, usually at a bar in

North Sydney or Crows Nest after work. She'd never travel over the Harbour Bridge anymore.

Phil met Rusty one afternoon in 2017, two months after Fiona's son turned 11. Rusty had returned from playing with his classmates at the oval close to school, a couple hours after the final bell rang, when their paths collided.

Fiona was petrified. She didn't want Rusty to feel like he was being replaced, or that Phil would be supplanting his father.

She and Phil were twiddling their thumbs at the back of Fiona's St Ives townhouse, waiting to hear the latch on the front door flip open. Phil stepped into the corridor once they heard the keyhole click, and he greeted Rusty with a fist bump. Fiona, four paces behind Phil, made a hopeful grin, but grimaced on the inside. Rusty met his fist with Phil's, and Fiona breathed. She and Phil returned to the kitchen, and cracked a bottle of wine.

6

Rusty's Dad

October 2022

Dad was never getting invited to Mum and Phil's wedding.

I'd see him often in primary school. Alternating weekends, and for sleepovers during the holidays. Going to boarding school made it tough to see him. Or anyone outside the Clarendon ecosystem, for that matter. But there now was a bigger obstacle to seeing him regularly.

Kids. More kids. At the age of 51 – the start of last year – his new wife had given birth to twins. Gioia and Mia. Two girls. I never heard about the wedding. Dad's wife – his third – was Bella, a Sicilian woman in her late 20s with dark olive skin, brown eyes, and broad shoulders, who had been groomed for motherhood her entire life. I'd only met her half-a-dozen times, but she would still squeeze my cheeks and coddle me as if I were her own. Gioia and Mia were her first kids, and second and third for Dad. It was new for both of them. There was very little time for anything else, including other children from previous marriages. I'd sometimes come by for a quick lunch, but I was usually only given a stop-in for coffee when it suited them.

Dad had always been laid-back about people coming and going from his place, offering his bed for me on sleepovers, or getting my Zia Sofia – who had lived with my Zio Giovanni (her husband) and Dad for about 20 years – to cook for me at a whim.

This all changed after Bella's arrival. She moved in with Dad promptly after the proposal (which was quickly followed by the marriage, I'm led to believe), and immediately left her longtime receptionist job at the aged care clinic in Lilyfield. She had turned one of Dad's abandoned closets into her personal wardrobe, fitting it with a mirror the length of the door, and installed a makeup table and vanity mirror in the other corner of the bedroom.

They had pushed the bed to one side to make way for a mini nursery when the twins were born, but they were moved into my old, vacant bedroom weeks later.

I met my new stepsisters a couple of weeks after Mum's wedding. It was still the start of the school year, so I didn't have any sport on Saturday. I also needed a distraction from the never-ending stream of photos from Phil and Mum's snorkelling adventures on the Great Barrier Reef.

I packed my rugby bag with some extra clothes and set out to Leichhardt. It took two buses to get to the town centre, which left just a short walk to Dad's house. Bella greeted me with a wet kiss and a bone-crunching hug on arrival, but the glazed look behind her dark brown eyes told me she wasn't keen on company.

Dad was sitting on the extra-cushy, green sinkhole couch that Bella hadn't been able to throw away yet. It had been there as long as I could remember, with Dad's position in the middle practically part of the furniture. The couch faced the analogue TV, on top of which rested an old Sony radio, with its two antennae sticking out at right angles of each other. Both seemed to be intact after six months of marriage.

Raffaele! Come sit down, have a beer, Dad ordered, without shirking his gaze from the TV. I sat next to him on the edge of the couch. Bella momentarily disappeared up the winding stairs, and seconds later returned with two passengers. Gioia sat in a sandy front pouch baby carrier, with Mia in the back. They were both asleep. Bella carefully, with the precision of a new mother, lowered Gioia into my arms, setting her out in a very cautious position. *Keep one arm at the bottom and do not touch the top of her head.*

I wondered how they'd find growing up in this house. And what sort of role I would have in their lives. I wondered about Bella. She used to be so loud, even annoyingly so. She'd put on bright pink lipstick, wore fluorescent overshirts and colourful cardigans (yellow and lime green usually) and would never sit down. Now, she looked so tired.

Bella would still project her voice so that, even if you were at the other end of the room, you could so clearly make out what she was saying, even if you were in conversation with someone else. Her verbosity would rarely be pushed onto Dad. He was the only one who wouldn't be routinely at the end of a short-tempered remonstration, though that wouldn't excuse her from projecting her foul moods his way.

The kitchen is a mess Vincenzo, I get no help around here. The babies are up again... why aren't they sleeping? They should be sleeping!.

Dad didn't seem much different. He didn't work Saturdays, so he'd often spend the day on the sinkhole couch or on the Bunnings chair on the back landing, sipping on Peronis, eating whatever Bella made him, reading La Fiamma, and listening to the radio. He had spent his weekends like this for what felt like my entire life.

When he wasn't married, he'd stroll down the road to grab a beef kebab or find some ravioli to put on the stove. But today, as a husband, he could rest easy. While Bella didn't rest at all.

How's your mother? She's got married? Good guy? Good. Dad spoke directly, and never for long. *Sit down, get a drink.* Bella was the one bringing over the drinks. Red Peronis, or Cokes.

In her mind, Bella was doing what she was meant to be doing. Her mother brought Peronis to her father all her life, her mother's mother did the same, and her *bisnonna* did the same, albeit back in Italy, and they probably weren't Peronis. She couldn't imagine her life being any different.

I told Dad about the wedding. Being a groomsman, being paired with Barry, standing in the little chapel near the harbour, and the reception. He shrugged most of the time or gave a disinterested nod. The only way I knew he was listening. *All went well? No incidents? They're Irish, yes?* He grimaced.

Dad always tried to undercut stories he wasn't involved in. He did this for school concerts, or birthdays he couldn't make. *Were you in tune?* It was his way of salvaging the burgeoning gap between his life and his family's. Knowing this, I shook my head at the suggestion of a punch-on between a bunch of loud, drunk Irishmen.

I didn't say anything about the honeymoon either, although I could feel my phone pinging with new photos at that very moment. He didn't ask, I didn't tell.

I asked him about Bella and the twins. He was hardly forthcoming. Bella left her job about three months before Mia and Gioia were born. *Seven and eight pounds each - beautifully healthy babies.* She had turned her back on the workforce since. Dad seemed supportive, given he spent most of his days in a factory, boat, jobsite, or unloading something onto a truck. But it put an extra burden on him. Already in middle age, I got the sense that working even harder for the next 20 years wasn't part of his plan. It didn't look like much would be changing until the twins were fully grown.

Bella stepped back into the house with a basket full of sun-dried clothes, which she heaved into her bedroom and dropped on the floor with a thud. Dad paid no attention. *How's school going? Are you still doing well? It's so important you do well. Are you still boarding? Are the other kids treating you well?.*

***

Dad had been to Clarendon once. Year 7 orientation day. Mum went with Phil to a conference on the Gold Coast, so she asked Dad to come with me. He never had much of a career to speak about, so taking a day off was never a big deal. He just shrugged and waved his hands if you asked him what he did for a living.

Dad rocked up to the school gates in a dishevelled tracksuit. His thin, stainless-steel chains smacked against the frayed Fila zipper, with his tweed-patterned hat (we just called it the old man Italian hat) covering the thinning hairs on his dome. I claimed him at the gates before one of the Anglo parents could redirect him to the Catholic school on the other side of Hunters Hill.

This is a good school, you'll do well here. You thank your mother's boyfriend for me. I had already been boarding at Clarendon for a month at the time, and I wasn't so sure. I'd met most of the parents already; there was the Year 7 parent-student church service, the Friday night icebreaker, and even a father-son dinner at a steak and ribs joint in the city.

Mum went to the chapel service with me, I skipped the icebreaker event, and Phil took me to the father-son event. Not that he claimed to be my dad. I counted the bemused looks from my classmates, most of whom couldn't fathom the idea of their mum with any other person but their dad.

Dad was impressed. He asked my Housemaster three times how I was doing at school, and assured him that I would behave myself. I was used to being embarrassed by him. He never had a filter. He said what he thought.

I think it intimidated some of the Anglo parents. The well-dressed professionals. Who had to take the morning off work. *For this shit.* They were dragged along in a sports car, Porsche or BMW, by their trophy wife, who'd put on lipstick and a short-fitting skirt for the occasion.

Then there were some of the more loose-fitting ones, those who probably hadn't gone to Clarendon, let alone third or fourth-generation students. They wore washed denim jeans, a polo or dress shirt and Dunlop volleys or skate shoes on their feet.

They would diverge from the suits but keep their distance from the wogs. Their wives were the mirror image, well-dressed but not manufactured like the trophies. This was what you'd see in St Ives. It was Mum, and it was Phil.

Then the wogs. Or, in the case of the Year 7 Anglosphere, Dad. He'd wear sandals over sweat-stained socks, which did nothing to hide the ashy skin colouring his ankles.

Any subtle hint I gave for Dad to hide his Catholicism wasn't heeded. He kept his thick gold rings on his fingers, bracelets on both his wrists, and puffed out the two chains on the front of his tracksuit, both leading to Jesus' lifeless body hanging on the cross. The chains rocked and screeched against each other, and Dad's sandals scraped the pavement with every step he took.

The thick, black hairs on each of his knuckles had been hidden under his rings, which were still more jarring than his permanently bruised thumbs. The chains thrashed and bashed with every pace. It was a particularly windy day.

7

Growing up in Clarendon

October 2022

Dad's a character, Patterson commented after the Year 7 orientation was over, smirking while he said it. I drew a breath, then responded. *Yep*. Exhale.

Boarding wasn't easy. While most 12 or 13-year-olds were starting to understand social cues and manoeuvring, very few knew how to execute them yet. This made for a cesspool of teasing, insults, and attacks, all because of difference. Conformity was king. A funny name meant you were playing catch-up from the start of Year 7. That was me: Raffaele Leonardi.

But perception can change. And the perceived truth is never permanent. This was great, because while you might have to put up with a ton of shit while you were at school, you were only there for six or seven hours every day, and then you could go home. To a more civilised place. Hopefully.

Boarders don't go home. Boarders are trapped in the school gates for 24 hours a day, five days a week. They liked keeping you there for as long as possible, especially in Year 7. *To get you familiar with our House culture,* Patterson said. My feeling was more that, and this had been affirmed over the last four years, exposure to the outside would breed contempt for the inside, which was bad news for the House.

I was the wog. Slightly darker skin, some wispy sideburns and a thin moustache cropping on my top lip. The sounding board for all Family Guy accents. The boarders got in on this, but they had other points of difference they also wanted to raise.

I was from the city and wasn't Anglo. Even some of the other guys from the city thought this was a bit weird. I didn't sneak out with them at night, making me a prime target for their pranks.

Screaming in my ear when I was asleep, throwing my textbooks out the window, stealing my weekend leave slips. They were annoying, sometimes infuriating, but I never gave them the satisfaction. They resented that I could leave school on a Friday night or Saturday morning, while they were held ransom until school holidays freed them from Hunters Hill.

I made my first friends by bonding over difference. Benny had come with his parents from Tel Aviv a couple of years ago. His dad had gone to Clarendon, and had moved the family back to Sydney especially for him.

Boarding was the real experience, Benny's father had told him. The rest of his family lived ten minutes away, in a recently purchased three-storey mansion on the Lane Cove River.

He was Anglo, but once he explained that he was from Israel and could speak a little Yiddish, he was the Jew of the House. Accuracy didn't matter. Distinction was paramount.

Eliot had it tougher. His parents left Vietnam when they were young to escape the war, and put down roots in Cabramatta. They now lived above their family restaurant, opened by Eliot's grandparents, on the back end of the local high street.

Eliot started Year 7 the year before Benny and me. He was the chink, the gook, whatever. On the surface, he didn't take much stock of it all. But he'd always be the first to leave for home on Friday afternoon.

The wog, the Jew, and the gook walk into a boarding school full of Anglos. The punchline? The English are the ones deciding who the Aussies are.

8

Bringing up Clarendon

March 2018

Fiona had no interest in sending her only child to boarding school. As much as she thought Rusty wouldn't want to leave St Ives, Fiona was also concerned about how she would cope without her son around. Rusty had been her companion in difficult times, and, she thought, her best friend.

But here Phil was, late on a Tuesday night, pitching the idea to her. Clarendon College. Fiona knew of the school. She could make out the sandstone buildings, reminiscent of a medieval castle, each time she drove over the Gladesville Bridge, usually after collecting Rusty from his father's house. But beyond that, she didn't have a clue. They had always planned on Rusty going to St Ives High, along with the rest of his friends.

Phil made a compelling case. Fiona conceded that it did look like an exceptional school, and one where Rusty could thrive, but sending him to board was intimidating. She had read about the antics and buffoonery that happened at some private schools and didn't want Rusty to be exposed to any of this. He was such a gentle boy, who was finally settled in St Ives.

Phil had been living with Fiona and Rusty for two months before he proposed Clarendon. Fiona thought their living arrangement was going smoothly. He was a great help around the house, often keeping affairs in order, even picking Rusty up from school, while Fiona kept her business humming. He would cut up oranges for Rusty and his school friends each afternoon they'd play AFL on the oval. Fiona thought this was a beautiful gesture.

Phil reckoned boarding school would give Rusty the sense of brother-hood he missed out on as an only child. He also said, though being care-ful not to lead with it, that the move would be good for him and Fiona. Moving into an up-and-running family household forced Phil to mould himself into Fiona and Rusty's lives, giving him and Fiona's marriage lit-tle space to blossom. They could make more time for each other with Rusty out of the house during the week. He thought they could make their own traditions together. Trivia nights on Tuesday, walks through the national park on the weekend. Fiona understood his point, con-fronting as it was.

Fiona knew Rusty wouldn't want to go anywhere but St Ives High. It was a tough conversation, but her son eventually conceded once he saw that his mother and Phil had already made up their minds. Fiona alerted Vincenzo about the decision once Rusty was officially enrolled at Clarendon. She and Phil had agreed to split the school fees; she didn't ask Rusty's father to contribute.

Sending Rusty to boarding school was bittersweet for Fiona. She could see that the change intimidated him, as it worried her, but she felt optimistic about her son's future at Clarendon.

Rusty would usually come back to St Ives every second weekend. Other times he'd stay at Clarendon, building camaraderie with the other boarders in his dorm. He would meet his old friends at the oval on Sundays to play AFL, but he was now an outsider to them. His friends from primary school would make jokes about Clarendon and embellish stories about their newfound freedoms at the more relaxed St Ives High.

Rusty looked defeated each time he returned home from the oval. Fiona would cook a hot meal for him, before Phil drove him back to Clarendon. Rusty was too considerate to burden his mother with his feelings. From time to time, Fiona could hear him sobbing in his bedroom after Sunday dinners, just before he would return to school. He would cover his face with a pillow, and wedge his desk chair under the doorknob so that nobody could come in.

Fiona wasn't surprised that Rusty was homesick. She thought he would settle into boarding school soon enough.

She didn't expect him to ask if he could leave Clarendon, six months after starting there. Fiona dismissed his question, reminding him of the opportunities the school offered, and how he would come to enjoy the boarding house soon enough. She started to worry about Rusty. Her faith in Clarendon was being tested.

***

Fiona felt guilty about it, but she and Phil's relationship flourished with Rusty away.

Their Tuesday evenings, as Phil had suggested, became reserved for pub trivia. They were part of the Smarty Pints, a team made with a few other parents from Rusty's primary school, who were the perennial winners of the $50 beer voucher up for grabs at the St Ives Hotel each week.

They'd spend their weekend mornings on hikes through the national park, and their summer afternoons lazing at the beach in Mona Vale. Phil, who didn't work as often as Fiona, thought he could install a plunge pool in their backyard. He had already transformed Rusty's bedroom into his own study. Fiona didn't mind too much. She was just glad he had something to keep him busy.

Phil proposed to Fiona after a romantic dinner at the Opera House. They had never seriously discussed marriage before. Phil assumed it was what she wanted, given they had already started a life together. Fiona hadn't given it an awful amount of consideration. But she said yes to Phil in an instant.

Just like when they met, Phil had caught Fiona by surprise. Then she worried about Rusty. Looking after her son was always Fiona's greatest concern. He was such an understanding boy. She prayed he would be supportive of her new marriage.

9

Stretched from both sides

October 2022

I tried really hard to enjoy boarding school. I stayed over the weekend at least once a fortnight, did all the bushwalks and bowling nights they'd organised, and smiled for their photo opportunities. Mum and Phil had turned my bedroom into a study once I started at Clarendon. They didn't seem to notice my absence anymore.

I was making some headway with the other boarders, but it never came easy. I didn't wear collared work shirts, care for the girls on their Instagram feeds, and tried to do my schoolwork on time.

I was an in-between at home too. My friends from primary school didn't look at me the same. *What's it like wearing a tie to school? Are there any billionaires in your year? What about the boarding houses? I bet a ton of shit goes down there.* I was being squeezed from both sides.

I'd still come down to the oval on Sundays. The footy games had gotten bigger since I left for Clarendon but had otherwise stayed the same. They normally played after school, so I hardly had a chance to play.

I craved the informality. It used to be a given that we'd meet at the oval once the final bell rang. Homework was an afterthought. No one wanted to or dared get in our way.

At Clarendon, we had to get our permission slip signed to go down the road. Presented at least six hours before we intended to leave. Even kicking a footy wasn't easy. The ovals, even some of the quadrangles, were booked for rugby training or another co-curricular activity in the afternoons. The exception was on Fridays, but by then I was ready to go home. I couldn't just walk down to the local ground, 200 metres from the school gates, because that would require a leave pass.

While I was grappling with this, my old friends were revelling in their newfound independence at St Ives High. *They don't care if I don't rock up for class, they couldn't give a shit.* I would hear the war stories each time I caught them at the oval. *They'll see us kicking the footy from the classroom, and won't say anything. We don't even need to go to detention either. They don't actually have the power over us. They can't enforce shit.*

I was so jealous. So much so I asked Mum if I could leave Clarendon halfway through Year 7.

Don't be silly Rusty, do you know how good this opportunity is? And the sort of strings Phil had to pull to get you into the boarding house?! You might not like it yet, but I know you're going to end up loving it. You don't want to go to St Ives, Clarendon is much better.

Clarendon pushed most my friends out of my life. I had a new life, and I was told to enjoy it. The wog had to make friends with the Anglos, the only childs, the kids of the wealthy parents who don't give a shit about them, and the rough-on-the-edges, corn-fed country kids.

Give and take. Give where the jokes edge on endearment, take when the chance is there. *Don't talk about my family, at least I'm not from a broken home. How many crocs you wrangle this morning, Steve? Did I just hear the Jew talk about money?* I didn't like the words that fell out of my mouth. The early years were a war of attrition, the best weaponry being those from the tongue. And stoicism. Any show of weakness would be disastrous. Retreating to a safe house on the weekends was my trump card.

Benny's parents hired a full-time nanny for him and his sister because his dad was always travelling back to Israel for work. So even when he could go home, there was never anyone there for him. I invited him to spend weekends in St Ives with me. Mum had to call his parents for permission, and Patterson needed the sign-off from both sets of parents before Saturday morning. It was different outside Hunters Hill. You could speak to someone without the fear of an insult being hurled back at you.

Imagine if I actually was Jewish, Benny would say to me. He never asked for an apology, and I don't think I was equipped to offer one. Despite feeling terrible about the things I had said to him. I found him crying in his dorm a few times in Year 7. When he ditched roll call before bed. His leave passes would be revoked as punishment, but he never had anywhere to go.

I'd shut his door and throw a pillow next to his head. He'd be lying on his mattress in the fetal position, with his hands clasped together on his chest, or blocking his face from being seen. I'd never say anything. I'd just shut the door and sit in the hallway by his room, or at his desk until he told me to go away. There were times when I started doing some of his homework for him. If I was becoming impatient.

10

In the House

October 2022

Benny didn't make it to Year 9. He went back to Tel Aviv during the summer holidays, without a lick of goodbye or see you later. I assumed he left with his family but didn't know for certain. *This place just got a little bit cleaner*, one of the Mudgee boys said when Patterson told us. He muttered it to no one in particular.

The jostling of social ranking had settled by the start of Year 10, and I was in a comfortable nook at the bottom. Occasionally insulted, but generally respected. Then Branderson, my knight in shining gym shorts, noticed me on my way to class, a few inches taller and with some muscle on my arms. My guardian angel, at least in his eyes.

I was ordered to the front dining hall table that very night, next to the prefects and rugby players. I had first go at the buffets, and I could leave school whenever I wanted. If it was for something sports-related, I was told.

I started to come home on random weeknights, surprising Mum and Phil each time I rocked up unannounced at home. I'd tell school I liked the physio in Wahroonga best, and that it'd be easiest to stay at home those nights.

Appointment at 6 o'clock, I said, but I'd be home for dinner by seven. I'd never seen a physio in my life. They didn't care. I was the top try scorer for first grade in my debut season. No signatures were needed, let alone a permission slip.

Mum and Phil didn't love it. My room, or Phil's study, had to be abruptly reconfigured each time I fabricated a physio visit. They wanted some advance notice of when I'd be back at home, but I ignored them.

One of Phil's bookstands had to be moved into the hallway to make space for my mattress. It usually rested on the back wall, just out of shot of any Zoom call Phil would take during the day. He would hardly work. My house before it was Phil's, I reminded myself.

He would never be awake when I left for school. I don't think he would even be up when Mum started her day. Consultancy seemed like a breeze. It afforded sleep-ins and after-school pickups, and didn't pay badly either. Consultants and redundancy packages were keeping Clarendon afloat.

The title was so vague. *Who were you consulting? What were you consulting about? Did they trust your consultation? What was the influence of your consultation?*

Equally vague answers were offered in return. *Business strategies, merger agreements, growth performance, etcetera, etcetera. Etcetera.* None of them, including Phil, seemed interested in the work they were doing. He rarely stepped foot in an office or had a connection with the rest of the workforce.

Phil joined the slew of other consultants and early retirees who watched us train in the afternoons. Branderson never liked it; he felt like he was being judged. Among the middle-aged men were old boys, board members, school council members, all of whom with a vested interest in the results of the footy team. Phil was none of these, but he found a way in, especially once I started winning matches for Clarendon. He'd try to avoid a label. *This is my wife and Rusty's mother, Fiona. He's a good footy player, isn't he? I knew he had something in him.*

Getting on the bus and walking through the school gates on the mornings I'd come from St Ives made me feel normal again. Seeing girls from other schools, sitting next to corporate zombies. It felt special to be commuting. I wouldn't see another Clarendon boy until I got to Chatswood. The blue and green tie made most of the suits on Mona Vale Road do a double take. They couldn't match the contrasting colours and khaki shirt to the school crest.

The mirage faded when I got to Clarendon. Returning to my dorm brought me straight down to earth. I'd dump my bags then usurp any queue in the dining hall for my second breakfast. Toasted sandwich and some cornflakes. Part of Branderson's nutrition plan for me. *No more muffins.* I always grabbed a couple before I left. He wouldn't find out.

The rugby season was suddenly over, which stripped my physio alibi from me. Year 10 was all but over. I got Mum to organise fake family events instead. Rusty's sister's birthday, end-of-exam dinner, my wedding anniversary. *Another year! Can you believe it?.* I'd add some personality to the notes.

These would just be texted to Patterson now. It made things a lot simpler. My standing on the rugby field made me untouchable. Aside from that one mattress flipping a few weeks ago.

11

One step forward, one step back

October 2022

Most of the wog stuff had come to pass by now too. Playing footy made me one of *them*. One of the boys. *The footy boys.* A good, reliable Aussie bloke. Within reach of the clubhouse, but on the other side of the door. Waiting for a trustworthy Anglo to let me in. Just like the Pasifikas – the boys from the Pacific Islands – on the footy team.

I lost all connection to St Ives. *Used to play gayFL,* I told Branderson when asked about my background, *but gave that up years ago. Game's fucking boring.* He smirked and patted me on the back. I'd wear my Clarendon rugby insignia like a tattoo whenever I was home now. Without a Sherrin in sight.

Some old friends would still be kicking the ball by the oval on the weekends. But most of them had moved onto different things. *Girls and pot,* Mum would tell me. She still found time to gossip. *Too precious and glamorous, those Clarendon mums.* She was right, but I didn't say anything.

Phil didn't seem to have a problem with their husbands. *Is Rusty's dad around? When did you finish up here? You didn't go to Clarendon? You're a bloody traitor mate!* He would offer a polite smile in response to their questions. Just happy to be included in the banter.

Next year I'd be getting my own room at the top of the house, right above my current one. It'd still be overlooking the quadrangle, but with its own kitchenette and couch. It was usually reserved for the house captain, but next year's wouldn't be playing first grade. He would be next to me. A small sink with room for a kettle, but no lounge and only a view of the hallway. A TV would look great by the bottom of my bed.

12

Term 4

October 2022

Term 4 had come around. Footy was out, rowing was in. The only sport with comparative esteem at Clarendon. I had to wake up 15 minutes earlier to get breakfast, and was relegated to filling out permission slips if I wanted to go down the road. *Like everybody else.*

Mum would still get me out once or twice a week. Phil had started texting me more, and drove me home from school often. *An old mate just started a boutique firm over in Drummoyne,* he explained to me. *Hopefully I'll be able to give you a few more lifts over the coming weeks.*

He was still an on-again-off-again consultant, but was set up with his own desk at this place. The suite included two lounge chairs, and a row of stand-up desks overlooking the Parramatta River. *Pretty sweet for a few hours of data analysis, hey?*

He started to ask personal questions on these rides. *Your mother tells me your Dad has remarried. How were your mother and him when they were together? Does he talk to you much? How's he with your Mum nowadays?*

13

The Banana Routine

November 2022

My room upstairs was under threat. From the rowers. *The fucking rowers.* Alistair, the giant cunt from Yamba, was being promised it instead.

He's getting rowing offers from schools in America, Rusty! We have to take care of him. I smirked at Patterson, and walked up to my room. If they win nationals, the room belongs to Alistair. Otherwise, it was mine.

I started drinking again. There wasn't much to lose at the moment. Patterson would breathalyse me when I got back to the House during the footy season. He'd go to sleep in my bed, and wait for me to wake him when I got back. He would only do this for the rowers in the summer months.

Patterson was a stupid man. I would never go back to school on the nights I drank. Mum would send him a text saying I'd be going home. And by the time I was back at the house, I'd be long sober.

The rest of the team never had to worry about this. *Relax Rusty, you've earned it*, they would tell me. Even Branderson would encourage it, as long as it didn't affect how we played. *Enjoy the rest of your weekends, get what you need out your system, and be ready for another week of training.*

The contradiction was astonishing. We were required to inhale every protein powder and trendy energy bar during the week, and would then drink ourselves to oblivion on the weekend.

If we performed on Saturday, we were invincible. Branderson would get the Year 12s to bring us to their parties, to celebrate as a team. The Pasifikas would never come along. No way.

The Year 12s would sort me with beers once I arrived at the party. It was always some sort of harbour-facing mansion with a tennis court or lush garden. Phil would linger in admiration of each house when he would drop me off. Once I had a beer in hand, they'd bring some girls over. Ones they had no interest in but thought I would. *Groupies*, the Year 12s called them.

At first I went with it. Kissing, sometimes more. Then afterwards, I'd receive bouts of unsolicited coaching from the boys. *Don't text her, don't follow her back. Nothing. They know what they're doing, don't let them think any more of it.*

I'd see them the following Saturday, sitting by the wooden fence of the school oval, just to the side of the grandstand. I never acknowledged them. Branderson, or worse yet some of the Year 12s, might notice. A couple of my teammates had girlfriends, but they were only exclusive during the week. *They know what they're getting into. They know what this is.* The glimmer had washed away by spring. We weren't in vogue anymore.

That was for the rowers. If they won nationals. We had to share the spotlight for now. I decided to keep my focus on rugby over the summer. Branderson wrote me a note getting me out of basketball, which allowed me to spend my afternoons at the gym, lifting weights and doing hill sprints. Branderson's assistant trainer, Humphries, would take us. He wanted us to call him Sam.

I didn't have much company at the gym. The Year 12s were finishing school and the Pasifikas never rocked up. They wouldn't step back into the program until April. It was just me and three others. Hamish, Sammy and Jono, who were all going into Year 12. I was the only one who had to be there. Patterson would check my room after school to make sure I was at the gym.

I learned of this when I was running late one afternoon. The teacher wanted to show that the final bell was for him, not us, so held us back a few minutes just to prove his point. I was getting back to the House to drop off my books and change into my gym gear. I caught him walking up the flight of stairs, turning off on the level second from the top, and peering into the room at the end of the corridor. He was startled when he saw me, one eyebrow raised and a knowing smugness on my face.

What are you doing? He was embarrassed. *Get to the gym now. I'll be speaking to Mr Branderson about this when I see him.* I knew he never would. I was in my warm-up five minutes later.

We had to be out of the weights area by 4pm. That was when the rowers would be finished with the ergs below us and be ready to lift. They'd throw our towels off the racks and onto the floor at 3:55. We wouldn't leave until four. At which point we'd be on the verge of a fist fight.

The worst part was what came next. The side exit pushed us onto the bottom of your average, vertical Hunters Hill street. You could hardly make out the sharp edges of the Clarendon gates from here. Only 100 metres, but a monstrous incline. Sprint, recovery, sprint again.

Until someone spews, Sam would order. My knees would push up to my chin on every stride. He'd be waiting for us at the top, adding extras if we didn't touch the school crest fixed to the centrefold of the gates.

These were the days when it was good to be a winger. And not Jono, the 120-kilo manchild with a beer gut and plenty of excess meat on him.

One could call him fat, but in the eyes of Branderson, a formerly overweight prop, he was an athlete. And always the first to spew.

So much so that Sam created a Jono clause. *We end when someone aside from Jono spews. Hamish, Sammy, or Rusty.* Jono didn't get it any easier though. There was one time when he started vomiting 50 metres into the run, whereby chunks of macerated chicken breast thrust out of his mouth, slipping down his shirt before settling on the kerb.

Jono refused to stop. He did the first time, but it was no use. Sam didn't give a shit. He'd have to do it again anyway, spew again, and again until it was satisfactory. The rest of us frantically dodged the remains of his lunch on our way up the hill.

Hamish, Sammy and I developed a strategy. One of us would sneak away at 3:45, and force two bananas, stolen from the dining hall, down ourselves. Small, but big enough for a reaction. If all went to plan, the remnants of it would be launched onto the asphalt pavement half an hour later.

We'd all jolt our heads the moment one of us spewed. Despite it becoming customary. We'd keep our pace, only slowing once Sam started pacing to the scene of the crime. *You're not done until I say you're fucking done, all right?* His words would ring through my head.

We'd continue, walking back towards the start line, until we heard that beautiful whistle pierce our eardrums. *Well done, go home and relax.* It was grim, but it was the best course of action. We'd normally be done by five if none of us could get anything up. We'd walk through the gym, give the rowers the dog-eye, then grab our stuff. I'd head back to the House, while Hamish, Sammy and Jono went home.

I didn't have much of a chance to visit Mum and Phil, irrespective of the physio excuse. I was busy catching up on homework after returning from the gym.

We'll be upping the ante on you boys this term, the teachers told us. *In 12 months' time, you'll be sitting your first HSC assessments. We gotta make sure you're ready. And that means at least three hours of revision every night, whether that be homework or study. No excuses.*

I was heeding their advice. Patterson was sniffing me out too. He'd pop his head in most nights, making sure I was at my desk and doing something that looked like study. He had Mum and Phil on speed dial, and I knew anything uncomplimentary would get back to Dad. Who'd probably show up at my dorm ready to kill if he heard I was dropping the ball.

Exams would be at the end of the term. That meant all the boarders would be hoarded into the language classrooms next to the House for forced study sessions. Phones were dropped into the plastic tub outside the rooms, one desk to a student, computers facing the teacher. Only speak when spoken to. We wouldn't be back in our rooms until 8:30, and were only given an hour before lights out. We'd enter the classrooms at half past six, straight from the dining hall.

To accommodate people like me, who were training most afternoons. This was shit for guys like Eliot, who spent their afternoons studying anyway. They didn't have sports or music teachers pestering them outside of school hours.

***

I went home for the first time in weeks on the Thursday night after exams finished. I got a leave pass approved after finishing an especially gruelling Humphries torture session. *Exams are over boys, so I'm going to really push you guys today. Cool?* Cool.

I left the House before dinner. I texted Mum from the bus, who got Phil to pick me up at the shops. *How's the offseason going? Are they pushing you hard? I bet they must be pushing you pretty hard.* Nod, nod, nod.

Mum wanted to hear about school. She was happy exams went well, and I was equally pleased there were no results yet available to corroborate my claim. I wasn't sure my marks would allow me to study the advanced courses for the HSC next year. Which I knew Mum wanted me to do. Out of my hands now. She called in sick for me the next day.

I got out of the study before Mum left for the office. Phil began working at about 10am, and stayed there most of the day. It was my first real day outside Clarendon since I started high school. It felt unusual. At a loss for what to do, I dug up the Sherrin in the back garden and headed to the oval in the early afternoon. I'd be there after the lunchtime kick-abouts, and hopefully spared a couple hours before school got out for the weekend.

I spotted my old St Ives friends as I made the final turn for the oval. They were lazing in the grandstand with a bunch of girls, wearing corresponding St Ives High uniforms. I went to school with a few of the girls, though I could hardly recognise them now. They gripped scrunched-up paper bags shaped like beer cans and bottles, which they would exchange and consume with every second breath. Goon bags rested on the torsos of the guys who lay in the laps of girls, sitting with their feet crossed on the metal benches and paved seats.

The others were at the edge of the grandstand, challenging one another to kick the Sherrin onto the scoreboard on the other side of the oval.

Right by where I was standing. I froze, panicked, and hid behind the scoreboard. I hustled home, hugging the footy with both my arms, hoping the purpose of my visit would also be concealed. Did they see me? I hope they didn't. They would've. One of them made eye contact with me, I felt it. A smallish girl with blonde hair, heavy blush and eye shadow. She wore an oversized, black t-shirt, ripped denim jeans, with long black boots coming up to her shins. The only one not in uniform.

Oi, is that? What the fuck? I heard two boys say. I didn't stick around for the response. I got home in five minutes, and spent the rest of the day lying around, lobbying Phil to order Chinese for dinner.

The rest of the weekend played out in a similarly reclusive way. Which matched Mum and Phil's plans. They would go for a bushwalk in the national park when the weather was good, or the mall if it was bad. Maybe watch a movie. It didn't interest me.

Phil drove me back to the House on Sunday night. *Have you heard much from your father?* He was still asking a lot of questions. *How's his new marriage going?* I really didn't know, was the truth. But I didn't want to let on as much.

Pretty good. Bella, his wife, is doing well too. She's really nice. Phil didn't know how to respond. *Makes a mean spag bol.* He frowned, then changed the subject.

Another big week of offseason training? I guess there's not much else of a focus left at school, now that exams are over.

He dropped me at the front gate and drove back down the hill. I waddled past the library and science building, then back into the House. *Rusty! Feeling better?* I nodded at Patterson, without changing my stride up the stairs. I had got back just in time for dinner. I thumped down the stairs and trod into the dining hall. Mash potatoes with beans and lettuce. Slapped onto my tray. I sat at the table furthest away from those rowing pricks.

14

Vincenzo and Fiona

June 2001

Like many Sicilian men, Vincenzo had a penchant for football and cigarettes. Only rarely would he indulge in both at the same time.

He'd been playing for his park team at Iron Cove Bay at the time that he met Fiona. Giovanni used to be interested but had hardly ever played after meeting Sofia; a Sicilian girl in her early twenties introduced to him by his mother. Sofia's parents were from a village close to Vittoria's, and had come to Sydney a few years before her and Alessandro. She had inherited the olive skin that reminded Vittoria of home. Their marriage, and subsequent children, were all but assured.

Vincenzo liked playing in the midfield. He loved to win headers, make tackles, and kick the ball forward. No other player was as desperate to do the dirty work as him. He paid no attention to the slurs. Opposing coaches would often just call him the wog. *Mark the wog, tackle the wog, push the wog. Do it. Now.*

There were plenty of other Italians on his team, but no others seemed to get the same treatment as him. The referees sometimes used his appearance to distinguish him as well, though never to his face. *Tell your wog player to calm down. The wog is one bad tackle away from a red card.* His teammates wouldn't stop it from happening but would never repeat it to him.

His footballing prowess made him a popular figure on the jobsite. He would keep a small, plastic football in the back of Giovanni's green BMW hatchback, which would be taken out whenever they could find space and time for a match. He would always carry extra cigarettes, which made friends of unfamiliar faces and brought important men onside.

He and Giovanni were often asked to fill in for workmates' football teams when they were a player short. Vincenzo would normally jump at the opportunity, while Giovanni would shutter away. He spent most of his nights with Sofia.

Vincenzo was approached by an apprentice one Monday afternoon in June. He played a weeknight competition with some old school friends at Sydney University, and wanted Vincenzo to come along. Vincenzo knew of the apprentice but had never really had a full conversation with him. He would chat over a smoke, but otherwise keep to himself.

Vincenzo borrowed Giovanni's BMW for the drive to Camperdown. He stowed a six-pack of beers underneath the passenger's seat, as an extension of goodwill to his new teammates. The apprentice said the games were just an excuse to drink.

The players all looked very smart. They wore matching navy-blue shirts and shorts, with yellow-and-blue socks covering their shinpads. Vincenzo wore a stained work shirt he only used for football and had stuffed ripped pieces of cardboard in his socks.

For every player, there were at least two friends. Vincenzo suspected they all lived on campus, given none of them were carrying car keys or a carry bag. They stood on the sideline, slowly drinking beers and actively criticising the referee. The game wasn't difficult; there were no rough tackles, and each player would apologise whenever they fouled an opponent.

Vincenzo subbed himself off halfway through the match, after he had helped his team to a 4-0 advantage. He stood by the metal bench on the sideline, keeping his focus on the game. Two fingers *tap-tapped* on his right shoulder blade.

It was one of the friends, offering him a can of full-strength lager. She was a short, fair-skinned woman in her early twenties, wearing a knitted green cardigan and a yellow beanie. She had blue eyes and already cracked the seal.

Vincenzo was embarrassed that he left his six-pack in the car. Nevertheless, he reached out for the lager, thanking the woman and sitting down on the bench behind him. To his surprise, the woman leapt over the rope to join him.

Vincenzo didn't hear the full-time whistle blow. He and Fiona – a 22-year-old accounting major living 20 minutes from campus – strummed up small-talk about the game, before discussing some more substantial topics. Family, work, culture. She started talking about post-modernism – the topic of her philosophy elective – before the team hurried them to the on-campus pub. Vincenzo welcomed the interruption. He circled back to his car to grab his cigarettes, which he and Fiona smoked once reunited at the pub.

She told him about her parents. Her mother was Caroline; an uptight, OCD-ridden woman whose sole project was her only child. She had abandoned her teaching job when Fiona started school so she could tutor her when she came home in the afternoons. She would revise what she learned at school that day or be tested on any questions she had answered wrong in a quiz earlier that term.

Her father Jack worked on the shipping docks. Vincenzo thought he may have worked with him before but didn't say anything to Fiona. He was in his early thirties but didn't want to advertise it. Fiona's father did anything he could to get his daughter ahead. He would work mammoth shifts for overtime pay and always put his hand up for weekend work. When he was home, he'd lecture Fiona about the importance of doing well at school.

Vincenzo thought it was a lot of pressure. Fiona only spoke positively about her childhood.

They became practically inseparable after that night. Their meetings would normally be limited to the weekends when Vincenzo wasn't working, but their phone calls became a daily, lengthy occurrence. He would often borrow Giovanni's BMW to drive to Marrickville, where Fiona lived with her parents.

Fiona's parents didn't approve of Vincenzo. Fiona said her parents always imagined her with an educated man. *A lawyer or stockbroker. A consultant. Anyone with a boring, white-collar job,* she would tell Vincenzo. Fiona's mother would put on a polite façade whenever Vincenzo was around. She always asked the right questions and would gently nod at each of his answers. Her father was more curt. Jack would grunt or scoff at anything Vincenzo said. His work, his family, and especially his relationship with Fiona.

They didn't prepare a seat for him when he was first invited for dinner. He was told to drag the garden chair from the front of the terrace to the dining table, which hardly had room for four people. The reception, especially from Fiona's father, disappointed Vincenzo; he and Jack worked similar jobs, which he thought could strike some sort of mutual respect between them. He knew the Anglo workers didn't fraternise with the Sicilians, but hoped an exception would be made when one was in your house.

Fiona didn't get a much friendlier reception from Vincenzo's parents. Their son was destined to marry a Sicilian woman handpicked by them.

Just like Giovanni. Fiona was invited for dinner on a Wednesday night, months after meeting Vincenzo. Her parents had been invited as well, but they never entertained any of Vincenzo's offers. As was usual in the Leonardi household, Vittoria was cooking penne Bolognese, using a sauce recipe from her mother. It was one of the few things she took from Sicily.

Vittoria set a plate of pasta in front of Vincenzo, Alessandro, and Fiona. They were eating on a cracked, formica table that had been in the house longer than Vincenzo had been alive. Vittoria refused to speak English. Vincenzo knew she was doing this to make Fiona feel unwelcome; his mother only spoke English when she needed to but had become a perfectly capable speaker in her almost 40 years living in Australia. Alessandro, who had become apathetic in his sixties, made no effort in conversation, only shrugging or shaking his head when spoken to. Fiona tried her best but knew her efforts were futile.

Their relationship continued to blossom, despite resistance from both their families. One year after their first meeting, Fiona shared a drastic proposition with Vincenzo.

She wanted to live with him. She was tired of having to justify him to her parents, who were concerned that Vincenzo would undermine her studies. Her final exams were coming up later in the year, which would determine if the top accounting firms would take her on as a graduate.

Vincenzo was surprised to hear what Fiona had to say. He had proposed marriage six months prior, but was swiftly denied by Fiona, who said she was much too young to be thinking about that. But she now wanted to live with him, which would surely lead to marriage.

Vincenzo thought about Fiona's parents. They would be incensed if they found out. The best place for her to be, they would say, was with them. The endless homeschooling Fiona endured as a child continued in university. Her mother would read over the course outline each week with Fiona, quizzing her on the key content and assessments.

But the idea excited Vincenzo. He was serious when he asked Fiona to marry him and was not put off by her initial rejection. She was still young, but he wasn't going anywhere. He knew that Fiona would grow on his parents, who wouldn't have any issues with her moving in. Giovanni and Sofia had gotten engaged weeks after he met Fiona and were to be married in two months. Sofia had already moved herself into the house and had been taking homemaking lessons from Vittoria ahead of her nuptials.

Vincenzo's parents had been trying to arrange his marriage for years now. They would settle for any wife he chose at this point. Even if this were Fiona.

He asked her a question. *What will your parents think?* She paused, then raised her eyes to catch his. She let out a laugh, nervously, and revealed her plan.

15

The Home Front

November 2022

Life at home wasn't what it used to be. When I popped up at the front door at the start of high school, usually for a public holiday Mum forgot about, it was barely acknowledged. Her and Phil were prepared to throw a parade when I got home on the Thursday night after exams finished.

We went to the St Ives Hotel for dinner that night. *Cooks a mean chicken parmi mate*, Phil reckoned. They came up here for trivia on Tuesdays, I was told, but rarely on a Thursday. The only times we'd go out for dinner were for one of our birthdays. Or their wedding anniversary.

Phil was asking me more and more about Mum's life before he was in the picture. About her relationship with Dad, if she'd had any boyfriends in between, if those boyfriends ever stayed at our place, how serious they were. I kept on shrugging them off, giving non-answers and grunts. Suggestive of something but definitive of nothing.

Was she close with any of your friends' dads back in primary school? Would they sleep in my bed? I didn't know. *I was pretty young, I didn't take notice of that. You don't have anything to worry about.*

There were times when I was palmed off to Dad for a few nights here and there, but I was never told why. Mum was good at keeping things under wraps. I'd be dropped off at Dad's, and picked up when she was ready for me

How are you, Enzo? Thanks again. Rusty's been really excited to spend time with you. I'll pick him up on Sunday morning – I'll shoot you a text when I'm on my way.

I was told it was Dad inviting me over. I don't deny this; he always welcomed me home. I just think Mum was strategic with the visits.

They'd usually be around a long weekend or school holidays. There were times when she went away, maybe by herself, but it was never totally clear. She always had her story straight. Except for the time I spotted a 'Byron Bay' souvenir-size surfboard lying in the back seat of the car, after I had spent four days with Dad.

It's for you! That's what she conjured, after a long pause following my question. *I thought you'd like it. I got it for you when you were at your fathers. Don't you like it?* She bombarded me with questions about my sleepover on the way home, presumably to stop me from doing the same to her.

16

Fiona

November 2022

Mum led a disjointed life before settling into suburbia. She was the daughter of two Scottish immigrants, who came to Australia in the sixties. *After realising how shite Scotland was,* Grandad told me with a grin. She was basically an only child. Her older sister, Tammy, died at 10 months, without a trace of cause or illness. Mum's mum – my Nan – found her in her crib, a cradled wooden basket handed down from previous generations.

Sucked dry, her skin was, with lips purple and cool. Like a plastic counter, Mum once told me. They refused an autopsy, and buried her at Waverley Cemetery three days later. Grandad went back to work, a labourer down at the shipping yards near Pyrmont, straight after the burial. Nan found work as a teacher's assistant in Earlwood a few months later. That was their survival plan, Mum reckoned. *Staying busy until it was their time.* That's until Nan fell pregnant with Mum, 10 years after Tammy's death.

She was the miracle baby and was treated as such. Nan started crafting an after-school curriculum for Mum once she was born. *To help her reach her potential.* She would be exclusively teaching her daughter from this point on.

Grandad worked overtime to pay for trumpet lessons and would always make sure Mum was behaving herself at school. Report cards were picked apart over tea, and areas of improvement were always jotted down. Holidays were spent at study camps or scientific adventures. Hikes through the Royal National Park or searching for new rock formations at Galston Gorge. Every day was an opportunity to learn, and they weren't ready to waste one. Suffice it to say she wasn't planned.

You could imagine their horror when she ran off with an older bloke while at university. A wog – the ones Grandad would keep a safe distance from at work. He had been made redundant back when Mum was in Year 12 and had channelled all his shame and disgust into determination to push his daughter to her limit.

Mum and Dad first crossed paths at university. Mum had been coming along to one of her classmates' football matches, mainly for the drinking at the end of each game. Dad filled in for the team on one of the nights they were short on numbers. They found chemistry over cheap beer and kept in contact from that night.

Mum didn't come home after an exam one day. Mum and her parents had been living in a small home, 20 minutes from campus. The exam finished at 3:00pm. Nan started getting worried at half past and called the supervisor to check up on her. The exam details were scattered on Mum's desk at home.

The supervisor didn't know where she was. Her paper had been handed in, and she was in the exam hall, but left like everyone else once it was over. Nan got to the hall by four and began trawling campus to find her daughter.

She said she would be coming home right away. Nan looked for her at the campus bar, and the gym. Nowhere. Grandad, who was pacing around the house, was called in after Nan couldn't find her. He joined the search, limping about to keep up with her frantic pace. No luck. They were ready to call the cops when they got a buzz just before dinner time.

I'm sorry. I know. I'm sorry. I'm okay. I'm sorry. Yes. I know. I'm sorry, I'm not coming home. I'm living with Enzo now. He picked me up from school today. I'm still going to study, but I'm also going to help out around his house. Just the normal stuff. His sister-in-law has loaned me some clothes, but I'll grab my stuff in a few weeks. When things have calmed down. I'll call you before then. Don't be upset. I'll call you soon. Love you. Tell Dad I love him too. Bye.

They had no clue where Dad lived, so they spent the rest of the night driving their silver Toyota Corona through Lilyfield, Haberfield, and Leichhardt, in search for his car – a green BMW hatchback. It was the only link they had to him. He'd been around for dinner a couple times, but they never accepted invitations to meet his family. They didn't ask where he lived either. *Probably with all the other Italians*, Grandad would mutter to his wife. The green hatchback BMW was the only lead to their daughter. The smallest needle in the Inner West haystack. Impossible.

Mum fronted her parents a few weeks later. By herself, ready to talk. Grandad didn't want to hear it. Nan wasn't too keen either. They didn't let Mum into the house. She collected a pile of her winter clothes, which Nan stuffed into the biggest duffle bag they owned and left on the doorstep for her daughter to collect. It was used for hiking trips the three of them once took together. It was to be returned. *Bring it back before summer. To the front door. No need to knock.*

Mum lived with Dad's family while she finished her final semester of uni. She worked a casual accounting job for a family-run firm on Norton Street. She'd split time between this and home, where my Nonna showed her the ropes ahead of an expected marriage. An Italian marriage. Cooking pasta sauce, keeping the house clean, spilling the gossip of Norton Street. I don't think Nonna was keen on having Mum in her house, but they eventually built a rapport with each other. To this day, she's never spoken badly about my Nonna.

While this was happening at home, Dad took any and all jobs that came his way. Never much of a career, not that that was the goal either. Enough to support a family one day.

They were married in a *very* Roman Catholic service three blocks from Norton Street. With seemingly every Sicilian in tow. My Nonno, in a very loose-fitting, grey pinstripe suit, walked my Mum, covered in golden jewellery and a traditional white gown, down the altar.

Grandad and Nan never returned their invitation. The reception was a massive party, I was told. *Lots of singing, dancing, and eating.* Nonno was old friends with Carlo, the founder of Bar Italia on Norton Street, and as a favour, got him to close the back patio on a Sunday afternoon just for them. The condition of his invitation.

Three years later, I popped out. Raffaele Vincenzo Leonardi, 7 pounds, 7 ounces. Camperdown, 16 September 2006. Raffaele to the Italians, Rusty to the Anglos, it quickly became. Mum had to fight hard for the compromise.

We lived at Dad's detached, two-storey home with the rest of his family. My Nonna Vittoria and Nonno Alessandro, my Zio Giovanni, his wife Sofia, and their two boys, Leonardo (born Alessandro but only ever called by his middle name) and Luca. I slept in the crib next to my parents during my first year of life, then was shifted to a bigger room with my cousins. In a little trundle bed, kept underneath their bunk.

Mum was back at work six months after giving birth. With Nonna and Sofia keeping the house in order, she thought there was room for another breadwinner around the place. She marched back to her office on

Norton Street, begged for her job back, and was told to return on Monday. They assumed she wouldn't be back after becoming a mother, and never really expected to see her again.

Monday caused quite a stir. *Where are you going? Who's going to look after Raffaele? You don't need to work, you have a husband for that. Your child needs you.* Her upbringing had sowed the seed for new problems. She never forgot what her parents did to support her. She needed to lead a life worthy of two people. For Tammy. What she was born to do.

And that's what she did. Working, as hard as two people. She swung hours that got her home before Dad each evening. She was determined to make something of it. She wanted more responsibilities, and financial independence.

Mum was made Accounts Manager nine months after returning to the office. This came with a bigger pay package, and she used this momentum to start pitching to neighbouring businesses along the strip.

She'd spend her Saturday mornings strolling up and down Norton Street, pram and Raffaele in tow, looking for work. She'd step into Bar Italia, kiss Carlo on the cheek, and start chatting. They were practically family. Mum, an adopted Sicilian, was more than happy to milk it. Chat to the grocers, grab some produce. *And just while I have you, who's doing your books?* Nothing wrong with being assertive, she would always say.

Mum set up her own business, *Italian Accounting Solutions*, two months after her promotion. She'd spend most of her Sunday afternoons (after church and lunch) trawling over the books of Norton Street. Her creative bookkeeping earned her a solid reputation among Leichhardt's grocers and butchers. Word of mouth, especially among Italians, became her best asset.

She started fielding calls from beyond the strip. Haberfield, Five Dock, the city. Sunday afternoons bled into Monday mornings, Tuesday mornings, anytime she wasn't working on Norton Street, or looking after me. Her days of wandering around the shops, using her child for social capital, were over. She didn't need it anymore.

The Sicilian women across Leichhardt, let alone her own house, started asking questions. *What's she doing? What's her husband doing? What about the baby? Who's meant to look after him?*

Mum didn't ignore their scowls. The women would be bringing down the washing or watering their front garden when she walked to work in the morning. Seeing a woman in a blouse and pants, even if they were just sandy chino slacks, was a sight to behold. Their bottom lip, Mum would recount, hanging a few millimetres lower than normal, eyes fixated on her every movement. Curious but cautious. And their stance. One hip in, facing down from their concrete landing. And their heads all over the place. Mum was sure of it.

Our front landing would be cleared of the washing before Mum left for work. She'd be up at 4am, taking down the clothes hung the afternoon before. This would be the earliest the clothes would be dry, no matter how still the night was. I'd be up at half past four anyway, making a fuss. She could tend to me by then. She took this off Nonna's plate, who was only sleeping five or six hours anyway. Sofia happily deferred washing duties to Mum. She was usually more help at dinner, which Mum was gladly absent from. It was a village within four walls.

Mum woke up to an horrific smell from the landing one morning. She had a full load of bed sheets and linen to bring down, a wash she only did every week or so. She had to beg Dad to put their bed sheets, sporting a yellowy tinge at this point, on the line. *They're okay, they're fine.* Mum wouldn't have it. *What are we going to sleep on tonight? What?* Domestic matters were one of the many points of tension in their marriage.

Mum waved the front light on, and immediately identified the stench. Faeces, from a cow or other barnyard animal, was doused along the rusted wrought iron fence separating the house from the street. It mustn't have been there for long. She only hung the bed linen at 9 o'clock last night. It smelt fresh, like it had just been pushed from the source. More likely from the fridge.

She pulled down the washing. Thankfully, none of it had been sprayed. She grabbed some rags from the kitchen, tiptoeing past the bedrooms, and splashed the fence with water, only stopping to brush off the bits of shit that had stuck to the fence. The worst parts were tucked under the paint, which had cracked after years of pressure from the sun. It had glued itself to the iron.

She scrubbed and scrubbed, even using cleaning fluid and a spare toothbrush to get it all off. By 5 o'clock, with about 45 minutes until first light, the smell was gone. The only evidence remaining was the soaked footpaths and stained water flowing into the gutter.

She didn't know who was behind it and didn't tell a soul about it. Not until she left Leichhardt. She got the same looks from the women that morning. She wore a matching pinstripe blazer and pants over a white, silk blouse her parents gifted her on her 21st birthday. She wore high heels, but only put these on once she was out of sight of home. She wanted to provoke the perpetrator, but not her own family.

A faeces attack wouldn't make her late for work. She hardly slept my whole childhood. She'd be working on Norton Street from 9 o'clock, get back for dinner at 6:30, put me to bed an hour later, and then start work for her own clients. Which had started to expand beyond her wildest dreams. She was thinking of bringing in another accountant to help manage the demand. But she was concerned this would undermine her employer on Norton Street, which she had an eternal soft spot for.

She'd focus on her own clients until 9pm, when the washing would be ready to hang. She initially kept the washing in the machine until she'd finished her work for the night, but Nonna said the clothes got stinky if they were left for too long. She'd now work until she heard the three *ding-*

ding-dings of the machine, which could call her to the front landing. It would take her 20 minutes to hang the washing, or half an hour if bed sheets or towels were involved. Then she'd get back to work.

Mum would finish her work when she was done. She'd roll into bed next to Dad, who was already snoring. Alarm set for 4am, ready to do it all again.

Dad didn't have much to do with me in those years. Or Mum, really. They both kept busy. *Get out and work, Vincenzo. Look after your boy,* Nonna would say. Nonno would spend most of his days in his frayed, wooden chair on the corner of our dining room table. A circular table with a linen tablecloth masking its decrepitude. The tablecloth had its stains, whether it be from pasta sauce, cigarette butts, or spilled wine. *It didn't make us look cheap,* Nonno would mutter from time to time.

The rest of his vocabulary was pretty narrow. *You getting work? How's your wife going? Look after her, always keep an eye out. How about the kids? You got to keep care of them, we're too old to do that now.* That was the general rotation.

Nonno was long done with work by the time I came around. They had paid the house off, but it was his body that forced him into the wooden chair. He never thought of a second career or got a second wind. Mum reckoned he missed the camaraderie at work, where he wouldn't have to speak a word of English all day. She told him only once that her father used to work around the shipyards. *A shrug and a raise of his eyebrows, and it was over,* she recounted. She didn't have much in common with Dad's family. Masquerading as a Sicilian was her only choice.

Dad followed his father's lead when it came to home life. He'd leave home before sunrise in search of a job, which could take him to the ends of the night. The shipyards or a construction site was where he went if nothing was lined up, where he could wait for an injury or accident to happen. His best work came when the workers were on strike. He and

Zio would be labouring from sunrise to sunset for weeks on end, charging as much as they could get away with. We could go an entire month without seeing them. *Working hard to put food on the table*, we were always told.

We knew there was a name for the workers like them. The one hurled at them by the union workers, who'd come to intimidate them at the jobsites. Dad didn't care. He could relax during the slower times. When governments and unions were in bed together, the Leonardi house was at capacity. Dad and Zio would spend their Saturday mornings on the back landing overlooking the unkempt garden, drinking beer and rolling cigarettes for themselves.

Nonno would keep to his wooden chair by the dining table. Often doing something similar. Sofia and Nonna would tend to the house in some way, usually shopping or cooking, or cleaning up after their husbands and children. Mum would be on the other side of dining table, crunching numbers for the bakery on Ramsay Street or an Italian realtor in desperate need of creative accounting.

Sofia and Nonna started taking me to the markets once I could walk. They'd get up at half past six on a Saturday, to make sure they were there before the stalls would open.

They taught me how to pick the freshest tomatoes and onions. *Hands, eyes, smell,* they would repeat. Sofia would defer to Nonna on questions. *How squishy does the tomato need to be? Should it be perfectly ripe when I grip it?* Every question was met with a detailed answer. Mum would join us sometimes. She'd be up by this time but already be behind her desk when we were ready to leave.

She's working too hard, your mother. I'm going to speak to your father, Nonna would tell me, whispering the final part. She never did speak to Dad, I don't think. Not that he would've listened. He was following his father's lead.

17

The Wedding and the Birth

June 2002

Vittoria was pushing her son to marry Fiona the minute she moved in. Vincenzo didn't resist it; he was just waiting for the right time. Leaving her parents was difficult for Fiona. She knew it would jeopardise her relationship with them but was surprised at just how swift they were to reject her. She wasn't welcome at their home, and they would refuse to return her calls and messages.

Vincenzo knew this would happen. Fiona's parents thrived on control. Under their roof, Jack and Caroline thought, she'd graduate university, and find the best job possible. Just as she was destined. Moving into a new home would be a disaster in their eyes. Vincenzo warned her that this would happen, but she didn't care. Or just didn't believe him.

Vincenzo re-proposed six months after Fiona moved in. There was no romance in his request. It was a simple formality at that point. Vittoria had been putting Fiona – with Sofia – in training to become the next Leonardi wife. She was teaching her how to cook, clean, keep the house fresh and how to spot the juiciest plum tomatoes.

Vittoria didn't like that Fiona had a job. The bookkeeping office on Norton Street was run by Alessandro Russo, an elderly man who had known Vittoria's father back in Sicily. He was idling in the front room of the office when Fiona walked in as a student, dressed in a seamless collared blouse and a long, dark skirt. On the advice of Vincenzo, she had already changed her last name to Leonardi. It worked perfectly on Alessandro, who was charmed by Fiona's initiative and offered her a casual position on the spot. His eldest son Andrea, who had taken the reins of the place, wasn't impressed with such an impulsive hire, but knew better than to question his father's judgement.

Housekeeping lessons were scheduled around Fiona. She graciously accepted Vincenzo's marriage proposal, which was mumbled from his tongue one lazy Sunday morning.

Neither of them had much to do with organising the wedding. That was left to Vittoria, who made the same arrangements that she organised for Giovanni and Sofia a couple years earlier. The Roman Catholic Church down from Norton Street. Any and every Sicilian invited. A string of gold rings and bracelets – the Leonardi family heirlooms – were draped onto Vincenzo and Fiona, the latter disguised as Sicilian for the day. The bride's side of the church was filled by groups of anonymous Sicilians who couldn't fit on the Leonardi side. Fiona was upset her parents weren't coming but didn't expect anything else. She kept her feelings to herself.

Getting married was the best day of Vincenzo's life. It was only bettered by the day he became a father. A sunny, spring morning. Vincenzo was on the back landing, rolling cigarettes for him and Giovanni. Fiona was planted to her seat at the dining table, watching Vittoria and Sofia cook a batch of pasta sauce after returning from the Saturday markets. She was excused from this excursion. The baby was two days away, and she had become immobile in her heavily pregnant state.

Fiona's water broke. Vincenzo raced his brother's hatchback down Parramatta Road, parking at Royal Prince Alfred Hospital less than 10 minutes after leaving home.

They bucked tradition. Unlike Giovanni, and his father, Vincenzo and Fiona snubbed the Alessandro moniker for their first-born. They wanted something new. Raffaele: an Italian name that could be appropriated by the Aussies. He would become Rusty to anyone outside of Leichhardt.

Vincenzo was beaming but did his best not to show it. His mother told him to keep his emotions in check just before they set off for the hospital. *Be strong. You're a father now.* Fiona was disappointed by his stoicism. He never was the animated type, but she thought that meeting his son would trigger some sort of joy in him. Only the faintest smile emerged when he first held Raffaele. After two seconds of contemplation, he returned his boy to his mother's arms.

Vincenzo wished he had a bigger part in Raffaele's life. But he knew this wasn't his job. He was to work and provide for Fiona and their child. His worst days were when he wouldn't even see Raffaele. Up before sunrise, home after dark. He never questioned it. His brother, who had two young boys of his own, didn't seem to share his feelings. Not that they ever talked about it.

Vincenzo would see Raffaele most on the weekends. Sometimes, they'd walk to the foreshore to get ice cream and count the boats on the harbour. When he wasn't being ferried to the markets or church. He hoped Raffaele would remember these moments when he was older.

Fiona was hardly involved in Raffaele's upbringing either. She had thrown herself back into work after giving birth, to the disgust of Sofia and Vittoria, who had become Raffaele's primary carers in his first few years of life. Vincenzo knew not to fight this battle; his wife would never shake off the pressures of her parents. The other women in this house wouldn't understand.

Raffaele inherited his cousin's school uniform a few months before he started kindergarten. The same colours Vincenzo wore as a boy. He prayed his son would have a better experience at school. Raffaele was blessed with his mother's perfectly-aligned teeth, and had smooth, thick hair that was brushed each morning. He would be at school with Giovanni's boys, whom he hoped would look after him. They were never bullied, which brought some comfort to Vincenzo. His other prayer was for Raffaele to have his mother's brain. He didn't yet know if this one had been answered.

18

Something Unexpected

November 2022

The separation was sudden. Only a few months before I started primary school. I had just been fitted for my uniform; a dark orange polo shirt with navy blue shorts, handed down from my cousins. They were still at Smith Street but were too big for this set. Mum took me aside one Saturday morning and said she wanted to show me something cool, down past the shops, where the library is. A surprise. I was getting ready for the markets, but she said I couldn't go today. She was carrying her work bag, a compact, black leather satchel. *It's at the end of Norton Street, by the busy main road.*

Nan and Grandad were standing beside their silver Toyota Corona, parked in a no-stopping zone on Parramatta Road. The trunk door was already up, and Grandad threw Mum's work bag into the car while Nan wrapped her arms around me.

How are you going? You're being very brave. Grandad was asking Mum the same question. Mum started to weep. This was something new. The surprise was then revealed.

We're going to live with Nan and Grandad. Just you and I. Mum spoke in a soft tone. *A new adventure.* Dad was going to stay and look after Nonna and Nonno. *You'll still see him all the time.*

I sat up front with Grandad while Mum lay in Nan's lap across the back seat. She looked exhausted. We arrived at their house after 15 minutes on Parramatta Road. They had been in a small two-bedroom terrace on Glebe Point Road for a couple of years now.

Mum's relationship with her parents had started to repair after the wedding. Her, Dad and I would be over every Christmas and Easter for dinner. Nan made a Sunday roast on steroids. Chicken, turkey, potatoes, veggies. And ice cream to finish. *If I finished my greens,* she would tease.

We initially had these feasts in the house where Mum grew up. A small cottage, squished by the similar builds beside it. Grandad would have to grab the deck chairs from the front garden to accommodate a gathering of over three people. They sold it after a big, fat number enclosed in a shiny envelope was slid under their door one day. It was from a suit, who wanted to turn the house into an apartment complex. Along with the two neighbouring lots. *Yuppie's paradise,* is how he pitched it to them. They used the money for the terrace in Glebe. And a six-seated wooden dining table.

The bed was already made for Mum and me. It was the mattress Mum slept on as a child, made with spare blankets thrown over an empty doona cover. The room was otherwise a hybrid of a study and storage room. Papers were gathered next to the walls, and cardboard boxes were stacked higher than my head.

Some of my clothes were there. Mum must've already handed them over. Grandad said we'd be able to go back soon to grab the rest of my stuff but couldn't tell me exactly when. *Soon, Rusty. Very soon.*

I hardly saw Mum that day. She stayed in Nan's room, not coming out to eat or tuck me into bed. *She's just tired,* Nan assured me. *You're doing so well.* I peeked through the bedroom door when Grandad brought her dinner. She was crying. The same way she was in the car. I went back to the living room to watch TV.

19

Growing up in Glebe

November 2022

L ife was different in Glebe. Mum was rooted to Nan's bed, in feelings of despair or overwhelm. Grandad slept with me for the first few weeks we were there.

My days were simple. Nan would be up early, around sunrise, to make us breakfast. Usually some toast, with avocado or a jam spread, and freshly squeezed orange juice. She'd put it on the dining table for Grandad and me, and make up a tray for Mum.

Grandad would take me to the park by the water most mornings. He'd sit on the bench next to the swings, sipping the coffee Nan had made for him. When there were enough parents around, he'd duck off to the reserve for a smoke, to the disgust of the joggers passing by. He wasn't allowed to smoke at home, so this was the only option he had. I didn't think Nan would be impressed.

Your mum just needs a big rest, Grandad would tell me. *She'll be better soon; she just needs some time. She needs you to be brave right now.* I would lend a hand to Nan when she went shopping, or was preparing dinner. I would stop Mum on her way to the bathroom every morning to give her a hug, telling her to bend down so I could kiss her on the cheek. *She needs you to be strong right now.* She had started to come out for dinner. This would be the only other time I'd see her all day.

The skeletons of Norton Street slowly fronted our doorstep. Dad showed up for the first time two weeks after we left. I heard his low, firm voice from the entryway, rising over the TV and scuttling noises from the neighbours in the adjoining terrace. I rushed to him, and he embraced me with a hug. Grandad didn't let him in. *Rusty's Mum isn't up for company.* He looked like he had come from a jobsite. Dirt and dust filled the tops of his fingernails, while beads of sweat had dried on the sides of his forehead.

Dad was as civil as Grandad was stubborn. He gave me another hug, then left. *Another NIMBY wanting my signature to protest the new tunnels,* Grandad told Nan at dinner that night. He shot me a look but didn't say anything.

Mum started sleeping with me after our first month. I got up before her most days and would tiptoe out of the bedroom to make sure I wouldn't wake her. *Important you let her rest.*

Mum quit her job at the bookkeeping office on Norton Street the day before we left Leichhardt. She renamed her own business *Premium Accounting Solutions* and had turned our bedroom into her office. Her clients were keen to stay on, despite the rebrand.

My focus on you will not waiver. I could rehearse her telephone spiel in my sleep. *I'm a Leonardi. I'm family.* This was to be her main job going forward, and she was already looking to double her one-person team. *An experienced Anglo,* she wanted. *Bringing some clients with them.*

She also had to find a school for me. My Smith Street uniform wasn't one of the items Grandad took back with him during his visits to Dad's house. These were brief, and he only took what was needed.

Those women aren't too friendly, he'd remark to Nan after returning. I'd be handed a load of t-shirts or socks, as well as some dresses and hangers to pass onto Mum.

I started at Glebe Public School the following year. Their uniform was a dark green polo and black shorts. I was able to keep the shoes Mum bought for me before we left. Grandad brought them back for me on one of his last trips to Dad's house. Too small for anyone else to use.

Grandad and Mum walked me to school on my first day. They perched next to me in the front garden, just inside the black wrought iron fence, to take a picture. They told me to keep my school bag on for the photo. It only held my *Cars* lunch box needlessly storing a packet of Tiny Teddys, and my broad-rimmed lunch hat. Nan, with her camera strap triple-wrapped around her wrist, waved us off as we walked down the street. She had trouble walking unassisted and didn't want to slow us down.

Mum started crying when we reached the gate. She had been crying less and less recently, so this caught me by surprise. I acted like I couldn't see it, and reached to hug her leg instead. Grandad patted the top of my head and squeezed my shoulder.

We'll be back to walk you home in a few hours, okay? I nodded to Mum politely. *Then we'll go and have lunch, and maybe Grandad can take you to the park after that.*

At Dad's place, smoking was part of the zeitgeist. Him and Zio would roll their cigarettes in the morning, often while the kettle was still boiling, and smoke them on the way to work. You could fish out rolling papers and filters between couch cushions, chair edges, under carpet coverings and inside bathroom cabinets. The smoke from the back concrete landing would permeate through the house on weekends, the smell rising to the tops of my nostrils each morning. They'd always be up early; their body clocks were wired that way and would probably never change.

Nan would kill Grandad if he smoked in the house. She never smoked. *Filthy, filthy, habit. And highly addictive.* Her rhetoric never changed. *Just drink water, Rusty. Maybe some lollies when your mum lets you. But even they can rot your teeth.*

Grandad kept his cigarettes, pre-rolled from the corner store, in two places. A little stationery box, hidden on a desk that Mum had now adopted. It was a small, golden box (very similar to a cigarette case), de-signed to store protractors and circle compasses. He did some rearranging to fit his cigarettes in there.

That was in case Nan found his main stash. This was hidden in a plain packaged box below his underwear and socks in his bedside table. *She'd never look here,* Grandad once quipped to me. He liked having someone in on his secret. Nan was already put off by his personal hygiene.

Any new cigarettes would be put in that box. He'd keep a lighter there, and another near the park. Under a rock next to the foreshore cir-cuit where the joggers would parade each morning.

Nan must've known he was smoking. I thought nothing of it the first time he ducked off for a smoke. I was used to the smell, which stuck to Grandad's body until he showered. But he never did it in the house, so she let it go. I suppose. I asked Mum if she knew that Grandad smoked. *A bit like Dad and Zio used to?* She laughed and walked back to her desk.

I still hadn't been back to Leichhardt. *Soon,* Mum would tell me. *You'll see Dad, Nonna, Nonno, and your cousins. Maybe you can even sleep over. We'll see.* I don't think she'd been back either. Grandad was doing all of Mum's communication with Dad and his family. I never knew when he went over. I'd only connect the dots when he came home with a car full of clothes and odd sods.

He'd never say anything to me. Only to Nan or Mum when I was out of eyesight. I'd pinch my bedroom door open or hide next to the door-way by the kitchen. *Vincenzo seems okay,* he'd say. *Misses you and Rusty.*

Still can't seem to get much out of his parents though. I told them he's started school, making friends. Vague with the details though. Nothing was ever said in return.

I was spending more time with Mum then. On the weekends mostly. Grandad, radiating smoke, would walk me home from school. Mum would be there when he was too tired but be back to work once we got home.

We'd do daytrips when she wasn't working. Luna Park, Manly, the Zoo. She would ask me loads of questions. *Do you like living with Nan and Grandad? Are they treating you okay? Are you making friends at school? Do you like their house?* I asked some of my own in return.

No, Dad won't be living with us. Not ever again. He has to look after his family.

20

The Day Something Unexpected Happened

September 2011

Vincenzo was rolling cigarettes the day Fiona left him. It was a sunny, Saturday morning. The week after Raffaele's fifth birthday.

As usual, celebrations were kept to the immediate family. Sofia bought a traditional cassata cake from Norton Street and topped it with fresh strawberries and jelly babies – Raffaele's favourite. They sat on the old picnic rug Vincenzo took to Tigers' matches, which sprawled across the grassy slope overlooking the bay. Raffaele was quiet for most of the day. His only show of excitement came when Sofia delivered the cake. This made Vincenzo smile.

As they always were on a Saturday morning, Vittoria and Sofia were at the markets, picking out the best plum tomatoes and ground beef to feed the family for the next week.

He hadn't seen Raffaele or Fiona that morning. He would normally find his wife by the dining table, reading over the books of another new client. He worried about how much she was working, but never wanted to interfere. Raffaele would often be taken to the markets with Sofia and Vittoria. Fiona must've tagged along.

The side door creaked open 20 minutes later. Sofia and Vittoria nodded at Vincenzo and Giovanni, who had rolled enough cigarettes for the entire weekend by now. Vincenzo was surprised that neither Fiona nor Raffaele was with them but didn't think to say anything.

Sofia started asking about Fiona once they were inside. She was unhappy about how little housework she was doing and thought – considering she wasn't buried in books at the dining table – she ought to help in the kitchen. Vincenzo inhaled another drag of his cigarette, and shrugged his shoulders when asked his wife's whereabouts by his sister-in-law.

He started to worry when he couldn't find Raffaele. His shoes, a dirtied pair of once-white New Balance sandshoes, weren't in his wardrobe, by his bed, or on the edge of the front landing.

Fiona must've taken him out. Her work bag was the only thing missing from their bedroom. It was a black, leather satchel gifted to her as a birthday present from her parents. They posted it years ago, without a card or any other acknowledgement. The only giveaway was the sender's address stapled to the cardboard box.

Perhaps she was meeting some new clients and was using Raffaele to butter them up. Like she had done when he was a baby.

Vincenzo got a buzz just before lunchtime. He had never spoken to Fiona's father on the phone before. Jack explained where Fiona and Raffaele were, and what was going to happen. Then he hung up. Vincenzo fell onto his bed and began to weep. He hadn't cried since he was a boy.

****

Fiona didn't have the strength to call Vincenzo that day. She lay in her parent's bedroom, resting her neck on a wide, plush pillow, while her mother Caroline cradled her daughter's head in her lap. Fiona seemed devoid of feeling. She showed nothing behind her deep blue eyes, which glazed over the cracked bedroom ceiling. Her face was hard, and her limbs stiff. She looked like she was drowning.

Just as Fiona had experienced when she fled her parents' home for Vincenzo's almost 10 years ago, her life was restarting all over again.

Fiona was filled with optimism for a future with Vincenzo when she was a university student. She was young, but Fiona wasn't naïve about the hurdles she and Vincenzo would face in marriage. Vincenzo knew about her parents, and the expectations Fiona was confronting. She also knew of the expectations Vincenzo faced in his life: to find a wife who would stay at home and give him children, and make enough money to support his family.

Fiona foresaw the issues that this would cause, but figured they'd find some sort of compromise that would allow her to lead the life her parents had carved out for her and allow Vincenzo to fulfil his duties as a husband and father.

It became clear soon after Rusty was born that this just wouldn't be possible. Fiona could feel the disgust from inside her household when, six months after giving birth, she stepped back into her blazer and suit pants, and returned to her accounting gig on Norton Street. It was fiery. Vittoria called Fiona a terrible mother. Sofia - who looked as enraged as Vittoria - assured her mother-in-law that she'd be calling Vincenzo to fix the situation.

Tensions softened over time. Fiona found ways to earn her keep while working a full-time job. She'd be home to bathe Rusty, put him to bed and put on a load of washing at nighttime. She'd be back on the front landing early the next morning, bringing down the load of washing from the previous night. She'd help Sofia and Vittoria cook pasta sauce on Saturdays, after they arrived home from the morning markets.

But Fiona could never truly embrace the role of Sicilian housewife. She came to this confronting realisation one year after returning to work. No compromise would release the burden of family expectation, for both her and Vincenzo.

Fiona was never meant to be a housewife, and Vincenzo was never supposed to marry outside Leichhardt. She would be a successful businesswoman, and Vincenzo would be a hard-working, God-fearing Sicilian.

Fiona grew miserable in Leichhardt. She started to think about Tammy. What she would think of the life her younger sister was living. If she would be proud of her. She hoped that Rusty would come to understand her predicament one day. He was being raised by Vittoria and Sofia as much as he was by Fiona. It made her sad.

Caroline was surprised to receive Fiona's call. It happened two weeks before she and Rusty left, on an overcast Thursday afternoon while Fiona was at work on Norton Street. Fiona didn't offer much information; she asked if her mother could collect her and Rusty from Parramatta Road, and if they could stay with them for a little while.

Caroline knew her daughter wasn't suited to being a wife. Much less an obliging, submissive housewife spawned from Norton Street. Caroline, who had softened in her older age, started to question her and Jack's parenting after their only surviving daughter ran away from home. She worried that, in their determination to raise Fiona the best they could, they didn't let her do any growing up of her own.

Caroline ran her fingers through Fiona's hair, tracing from the temples down past her ears. Fiona's eyes held the same emptiness that her mother saw when she slid onto the back seat of the Toyota Corona on Parramatta Road. Caroline was concerned for Rusty. He had always been a happy boy, she thought. She hoped he would forgive his mother for taking him from his father.

Two slow knocks were heard from the door. Jack's face emerged. He made a show of his phone returning to the front pocket of his denim jeans, and gave his wife a short nod. Fiona didn't seem to notice the interaction.

21

On The Road Again

November 2022

We were with Nan and Grandad for a year before we exiled ourselves to St Ives. Just as I was starting to settle. *A place for you and Mum*, Nan said, pinching my cheek on the day we left. The tears running down my face were swept away by her index finger and thumb. She let go, acting like nothing happened. Mum was scared too.

I first visited Dad's six months after we left Leichhardt. He'd arranged for me to spend weekends there once a month. I'd sleep in my old trundle bed next to my cousins. Nonna and Sofia didn't want me back at first. Mum and I had no respect for the family, we were told. I acted like I didn't hear it.

Some mornings I'd walk with Sofia and Nonna to the grocers. *How's your mother going? Is she happy with her life now? She's back with her parents, yes? I haven't seen her at work since you left.* I was told to keep my answers brief. *She's good. We're happy. She's not working there anymore.*

Dad always stuck up for me. He would take me to see the sailboats on the mornings I wasn't at the markets. Rowers would sometimes glide by, following the commands of a bashed-up dingy 50 metres away. He didn't smoke when I was over. Sometimes we'd go to the West Tigers matches, when they were playing in Leichhardt. He used to go with friends when he was younger. He hardly asked about Mum.

I just want you both to be happy Raffaele. You'll both always have a home here.

His second wife moved in a few months before my first sleepover. Giorgia. The one before Bella, as she came to be known. *A nice girl from a village near Calabria*, Nonna told me. She worked on Norton Street and went to church every Sunday. *Your mother hardly went to church, always working, never lending a hand. Do you have to do the work at your house now?*

She had long, dark hair, brown eyes, and olive skin. She wore sundresses at both ends of the year, and leather jackets and denim jeans in the middle. She worked at her family deli while she waited for a husband. Keeping track of inventory, some management responsibilities, on the floor when it was busy. The deli had been there since her family immigrated after the war. Her Nonno helped run one in Italy, before it got destroyed by bombers on the eve of surrender.

They'll be married soon, Nonna said. *A big celebration. Giorgia will leave her job and stay at home while Vincenzo works. How it should be.*

Dad's room saw some changes. The old queen bed had become suffocated by a castle of pillows (at least ten), and a makeup table had been fixed to the corner of the room, where Mum's square desk used to be. The hanger on Dad's side of the closet held the same mangled, stained shirts. Others in the closet folded on top of each other, and the rest were stuffed in a heap across different drawers. The red, plasticky carpet had been cleaned since I last saw it. Presumably when Giorgia moved in.

Dad wouldn't have changed the room after Mum left. He didn't have a reason to – he'd be up at six and only get back in time for dinner. He'd spend a few hours watching TV or smoking outside before he'd collapse into bed, or on the couch, before doing the same thing again the next day.

The room was compact, almost like a square. The bed bordered the length of the side wall and took up most of the floor space. One wardrobe covered half of the wall, ending next to the hinges of the door. He'd shared this with Mum. Giorgia pushed Dad's clothes to the end of the hanger and the bottom drawers. There was one small window, a wooden cross glued above the bed, and a fake rose resting in an old milk glass in the other corner of the room.

Giorgia wanted kids. Her own kids, that is. Moving to St Ives would surely end my welcome in Leichhardt. It made me sad, but I didn't fight it.

Dad and Giorgia had married about 10 years ago. Now, 16 years old living inside a sandstone castle, I would only see Dad every now and then. He never had kids with Giorgia, and I never became the threat I thought I would be. But boarding and living on the north shore made it hard to stay close. Christmas and Easter were the only real times I would see him. I still think we made it count.

22

The Last Week of School

November 2022

I spent the last weekend of Year 10 at home. The whole school, including the boarding house, would be on camp the next week. Then, school would be over. I'd be going into Year 11, hopefully with the top dorm in the house, at the end of January. Pending rowing failure.

Mum told me she'd pick me up on Friday afternoon, but I was stuck with Phil. More and more questions. *Your Mum said the other day that her company got its start with Italians needing to fudge their tax returns! How about that? Your mother, the mafia accountant.* He started to snicker. *Good value, right?*

Serious questions followed. *Where did you guys go after you left your father? Do you know if your mother talks to him anymore? Do you ever ask him about that?*

I didn't think it was fair that Mum was being so secretive about her past. Not that she could hide it either; I'm the product of it, as is her livelihood. But that seemed to be her way of survival. Suppression is the simplest form of distraction, no matter how obvious the subject matter.

Phil was still keen to hear about the offseason. I showed him where we did hill sprints, pointing to the exact area where one of us would cough up our lunch. He met me inside the front door of the House and was chatting with Patterson when I came down. *Big year on the footy pitch for Rusty!*, Patterson said, slapping my back and shaking my shoulders. Phil was beaming with pride.

We ordered a pizza back in St Ives, getting it delivered in time for Mum's arrival home. She was back in perfect time, exchanging the pizza and a begrudging nod with the driver as she closed the front door on him. She embraced me, then retreated to her bedroom. *Big couple weeks.* Phil was speaking softly, almost whispering. *Half-year reports, office shut-downs, all that jazz.*

He had done a big clean of the house in the time since I had been there. The destroyed Sherrins, which sat in the front garden next to the gate, were gone. They had been here for years, dormant since I started at Clarendon.

A wooden tub, carved into a hollow triangular prism, now shone from the front landing. In it were three clean, pumped Gilbert rugby balls, stowed away in a pyramid shape.

To stay sharp over summer, Phil told me. *When the school gym is closed.*

Phil was getting less and less work. The schoolmates that employed him said the job would be flexible, which meant he'd be asked to show his face at the office twice a week and be on-call for matters needing another set of eyes. A soft renovation at home was keeping him busy. I didn't know if they still planned on installing a plunge pool in the backyard. There certainly was no attic room for me yet.

Mum welcomed the distraction but never showed it. They were co-existing nowadays, like two housemates who'd be living by themselves if they could afford it. Phil turned his study into an actual bedroom for me as part of the home improvement project. *There's always the kitchen table if I need to work,* he reasoned to me.

The plastic foldable table that rested on the wall when I was home was moved into the shed at the back of the house. Relegating it to utter irrelevance, with the rest of the doomed items in there. He furnished the bedroom with two Ikea closets and a clothes rack on opposite corners, towering above my queen bed. The closets were empty, of course. My belongings were back at Clarendon, except for some clothes I'd keep for an impromptu visit. These were stuffed into the bottom shelf of the closet next to my window.

Mum emerged from her room in a pair of stained tracksuit bottoms, a grey hoodie and woolly socks, about ten minutes after she had got home. An interesting choice for November.

Premium Accounting Solutions had become a local bookkeeping empire. Like it was in Leichhardt, word-of-mouth was still Mum's best asset. She'd concentrate her business on local high streets, like she had done on Norton Street, focusing on the family-run businesses who didn't trust the big accounting firms. She'd sell her services for cheap, before upping the price when the referrals came in. Most her new clients were bakeries, restaurants, or newsagents north of the Harbour Bridge. St Leonards, Chatswood, North Sydney. Dozens of small businesses were on the hook.

She made her first hire while we were living in Glebe. Claire, a late twenties, early thirties woman who'd been at a firm in North Sydney. She convinced some old clients to jump ship with her. Mainly small businesses from Hornsby. Giving Mum her start in the non-Sicilian world. Now, she had six full-time accountants at her office in Crows Nest, with two casuals tapping in for the end of financial year and Christmas time. They landed their first franchise earlier in the year, an ice cream joint from Los Angeles that had opened a shopfront in Manly.

She always became distant during a seasonal crunch. She grabbed a couple of slices of pepperoni pizza, slapped it onto a plate, nodded her head at some polite conversation between Phil and I, then took herself back to her bedroom. *Usually just lies downs in the dark*, Phil told me. *Rarely falls asleep.*

She was a ghost for most of the weekend. She'd sleep long hours, and only leave her bed to make coffee or use the toilet. It reminded me of our first weeks in Glebe.

***

They were the final memories I had of Nan and Grandad. A heart attack got Grandad months after we moved to St Ives. He was by the foreshore when it happened. Two joggers found him crouched over a park bench, lying on his side, unresponsive, with a cigarette pinched between his index and middle fingers. They carried him to the playground, where the road was, and called for an ambulance. Nan heard the sirens run past but had no idea who it was for. Grandad said he was grabbing a paper and milk from the corner store in the other direction.

The doctors did everything they could to save him, Mum assured me. They rushed him into surgery to find the artery blocking blood flowing to his heart, but it was to no avail. He was dead before Nan and Mum got to the hospital. The doctors told Nan that smoking probably didn't cause the heart attack. It couldn't have helped.

I was with Dad that weekend. I had gone with Sofia and my cousins for gelato and had walked to the water to see the sailboats glide by. Dad was waiting for me on the front landing, dragging on the ends of a cigarette. I saw him as we turned the corner to our street.

You need to be brave, for your mother, Raffaele. His eyes were serious and didn't stray from mine. *This won't be easy for her. This is when you need to step up for her. It's going to be tough, but it's important, okay? You promise to be brave?* Okay.

I didn't understand what he was saying. Nothing had changed. I was still at my Dad's house, spending another weekend here, before I went back to school on Monday. Just like it was that morning. No different. So there was no reason to act differently, I figured.

Mum picked me up the next morning. Dad was waiting for her, sitting vacantly in the same place I found him the previous afternoon. He opened the front gate and met her with a hug. She didn't come in or walk onto the landing. Dad called me out, and as instructed, I gave her a long hug, squeezing her leg and the bottom of her torso. Tears were falling down her face.

Be brave, Dad mouthed to me. Then we left.

I learned what the worst part of grief was: its uselessness. All consuming, but utterly unhelpful. It certainly didn't help me be brave for Mum.

Nan lived with us for a few weeks after Grandad's passing. I wasn't much help for either of them. They would both fuss over me, probably to distract themselves. Nan would be up at sunrise, preparing a full breakfast spread. Toast, bacon, eggs, and the freshly squeezed orange juice I had once become used to. We never ate much, but she made the same spread every morning.

She'd only leave the house for the shops, usually grabbing a week's worth of bread, fruit, and milk. Mum, who gave her room to Nan, was sleeping with me. She never left the bedroom. Some nights I could hear her choking back tears, through quick jolts of anxious breathing or heavy pants caused by loads of snot and tears filling her face. Other times, it sounded like she was hyperventilating.

Nan would make Mum a tray when I was done with breakfast. She'd collect it an hour later, looking no different to how it was when she made it up. Except for the coffee mug, which would stay by Mum's bedside table for the rest of the day.

This was the holding pattern until the funeral. It was at a place 30 minutes from home, in a big purpose-built compound off the Pacific Highway. Dad and Giorgia were some of the first to arrive, fronting the steps of the cream-coloured hall in all-black attire. Giorgia wore a black veil covering the top of her face, and chinks of gold jewellery on her wrists. They hugged Nan, Mum, and me. We were told to line up outside the door and were reserved seats on the front aisle.

23

Localists

November 2022

A similar procession followed two years later, but it was just Mum and I at the door. Nan's death was much more banal than Grandad's; she was found in her bed by the cleaner, who would use his keys to let himself in every Tuesday. The paramedic reckoned she'd been dead for a day or two. Never any chance to bring her back. *Seemed to go peacefully*, we were told. We spent the next few months between Glebe and St Ives, sorting old clothes, books and belongings into cardboard boxes, and drinking tea or lime cordial on the couch. In a state of paralysis.

Mum seemed much more hardened this time around, like she had been preparing for Nan's death. She was familiar with mortality now, so she chose to act like it was living on her doorstep. Becoming friends with the hard things to stop them from ruining her. I couldn't offer a better solution.

Dad wore the same suit for Nan's funeral as he had for Grandad's. He left Giorgia at home this time and was one of the last people to leave the reception. He was standing by the espresso machine, chin-wagging with whoever gave him a second glance. He greeted Mum with a warm embrace, and a soft kiss on the cheek.

Mum sold the Glebe terrace three months after the funeral. She had no interest in moving there and didn't need a passion project. She found the perfect buyer. A 40-something Middle Eastern man, brandishing diamonds on his wrists and earlobes, representing an urban developer *very interested in your property*. He'd been door-knocking up and down Glebe Point Road for years. *But I've only ever had eyes for this place.* Mum invited him in, and he went straight into his sales pitch.

Perfect distance between the water and the shops, walking distance to the city, but with some distance from the rat race. It's a big lot, so there's potential to expand on the existing land.

Translation: we want to take a wrecking ball to the place, build as many homes as we can, and sell or rent them to the yuppie with the deepest pockets.

This area's just been re-zoned to promote property investment, so that flexibility is of a lot of value to us.

We're going to build as high as we want. We don't care who the tenants are, or what they do, as long as they pay rent at the end of every month.

We are prepared to offer a significant sum we believe reflects our interest in your property.

We're so sure we're going to make so much money off you, that we're going to give you an offer that no hardworking Australian family could ever compete with.

They shook hands two weeks later. The neighbours gawked when the development notice went up on the gate, which had turned orange with rust. The dominos were starting to fall.

Mum used most of the money from the sale to get ahead on our mortgage. She had only scraped enough for the deposit a couple of months before we bought the place and had been putting every lick of savings into the offset account over the last few years. Some of Glebe's proceeds were put into her business, which she was still trying to keep on top of.

The rest was for a week-long snorkelling trip on the Whitsundays. We flew in on the first week of June, when it was just starting to get chilly in Sydney. She complained about the coolness of the water, but I think she was just happy to be away.

Mum had no remaining links to the other side of the Harbour Bridge. She hardly ever left the north shore; maybe for the odd weekend outing or to pick me up from Dad's, but she had become very parochial. We'd only venture to Mona Vale on a summer's day. The other beaches were too far away.

Perhaps that's why Mum and Phil worked. They were each perfectly stale. He was raised on the north shore, and never really left. They'd never have crossed paths if Mum moved us to Glebe or wanted me closer to Dad.

***

Mum and Phil met over the phone. Phil was working for a Chatswood phone repair shop that thought they were paying too much tax. They wanted to sack Phil, who they said was giving poor advice.

He had to get them back onside. His company had already worked with Mum on some referrals, but he'd never had much of a personal link to them. He called her, negotiated some terms for their work, and finalised a deal. As it was in previous agreements, Mum's company would get no recognition for their work. Phil would tell the client it was under the consultancy's umbrella. A ghostwriter. She would crunch some numbers and offer ways to tighten their spending.

Phil insisted they go for a drink the day she handed in her final report. *As a thank you*, Mum said. Phil maintains it was a date. They never came to a consensus.

Any romance or giddiness I saw in those initial encounters between Mum and Phil was buried by now. They were an old, routine-ridden, suburban couple. Like the rest of St Ives. Working to pay off their mortgage and praying it would revive the marriage.

Phil drove me back to Clarendon on the Sunday night before camp. It would be the last night in the House for the school year. The Year 12s were already out, probably at schoolies by now, and the rest of us had camp to look forward to.

Annual House maintenance would start while we were away. There was already some scaffolding and tools lying by the door when I got back, which were left from the initial works over the weekend. It would ramp up once the holidays began, with hopes of finishing before Christmas.

Nothing they could do would brighten up the place. I knew that by now. Any chances of that, at least for me, rested in one of those rowers catching a crab at nationals.

24

Giorgia

October 2011

Vincenzo's family never spoke about Fiona or Raffaele after they left. They shrugged their shoulders or cursed under their breath when their names were muttered, but otherwise acted like nothing had changed. Sofia had returned Raffaele's school uniform to his cousin's wardrobe and tucked his trundle bed under the bunk. Forevermore.

Giovanni would sit with Vincenzo, as he did before, rolling cigarettes and drinking beer. He never said anything about the separation. Their father didn't think much of it either; he did his best not to broach the subject and would only offer a nod or shrug when his wife would come to him about it.

Vincenzo knew Giorgia by face, but never by name. She was easy to spot; the dark-haired daughter of the Calabrian family who owned the deli on Norton Street. She was slicing hams or bagging cheese behind the counter every Saturday and had gained a reputation for her charm and salesmanship. Vincenzo didn't shop at the deli, and would only see glimpses of her from the street. He thought she was attractive, but so did the rest of Leichhardt.

Vincenzo did a double-take when he saw her in his kitchen. He and Giovanni had been working 12-hour days on a much-delayed multi-storey office building on George Street at the time. The builders were desperate to fulfil the terms of their contract, which was in jeopardy due to what they said were lazy workers. Vincenzo and Giovanni negotiated a good price for their labour and had been working all-day on the site for weeks.

Giorgia was smiling and laughing with Vittoria, who was hunched over the stove and gripping a wooden stirrer. They were speaking about something to do with the pasta sauce, but both went silent once they heard Vincenzo walk through the door.

Vincenzo. Vittoria set the stirrer on the counter and wiped her palms on her apron. *Questa è Giorgia.* The guest extended her hand, palm facing the ground, to greet Vincenzo. He extended his forearm, covered in dirt and dried cement, and shook her hand. Giorgia paid no attention to Giovanni, who had stuttered in after Vincenzo and had already made his way to the shower. Neither did Vittoria.

Giorgia's intentions were clear. She wanted to be married, leave her family's deli, stay at home and raise children. She didn't see any merit in being subtle either. When Vincenzo wasn't being eyed by his mother over dinner, it was Giorgia looking through him. Vittoria had been scouting a new wife for her second-born the moment Fiona left. Perhaps even before that.

Vittoria had already been a victim of Giorgia's charm. The attractive, olive-skinned woman had memorised Vittoria's order and would have it prepared each time she entered the shop. Vittoria also had a good rapport with Giorgia's parents, who had come from Calabria when they were little. It wasn't too great a step for her to invite Giorgia to dinner. *To meet my son.*

Vincenzo was still shattered. He spent most of his waking hours thinking about Fiona and Raffaele, whom he had hardly been able to see since they left. Fiona's father Jack had dropped in a few times to collect some of their belongings, but this would only happen while he was out. He felt lucky to be so busy at work and was concerned about how he would manage once work settled down. Many nights, often on the weekend, he'd drink himself into a slumber. Other times he would sob until he fell asleep.

Giorgia was sharing Vincenzo's bed one month after they met over dinner. He was called back to the dining table after Vittoria had escorted Giorgia up the side path and into her car. Vittoria told him that Giorgia wanted to marry, and that she had assured her of Vincenzo's proposal. He didn't flinch when he heard her mother's words; he thought this would happen and couldn't get himself to care. This was the natural order of things. He couldn't defeat it. Giorgia would leave the deli and join Sofia and Vittoria at home. She would be a big hand for Sofia, who was taking on more duties as Vittoria became increasingly immobile.

Vincenzo shouldn't have married Giorgia. He came to this conclusion months after his second wedding, a small civil ceremony in Leichhardt, but years before they would divorce. She wanted to start a family. Vincenzo wanted his old family.

Giorgia resented Vincenzo's first marriage and did her best to remove any relics from a life before her. Vincenzo found a completely reshaped bedroom the day Giorgia moved in with him. His button-up shirts were pushed to the edges of the wardrobe rails, and his sandals were hidden out of view at the bottom of the cupboards.

Giorgia wanted children straight away. *At least three,* she would tell Vincenzo. She came from a family with three siblings who all had worked at their deli. Vincenzo had no interest in other children. Giorgia resented Raffaele. She hardly spoke to him on the few occasions he visited his father. One Sunday, she didn't make enough pasta to feed him. She said it was a mistake, but Vincenzo didn't believe her. He gave his plate to his son, who gleefully ate and thanked Giorgia afterwards.

Vincenzo would now spend almost all his weekend on the back landing, rolling cigarettes and fetching beers for himself and Giovanni. His brother hardly spoke to his wife or children, who were largely being raised by their mother. Giovanni never seemed upset about it. That's just how it worked.

Giorgia's appetite for children persisted throughout their marriage. She was upset by Vincenzo, who would ignore her sexual advances and refuse to touch her. He would only come to bed once she was asleep. Sometimes he would be drunk, other times he'd be upset. He would muffle his cries into his pillow, scared the noises would wake his wife.

Both Vincenzo's parents died during the early years of his marriage to Giorgia. They passed at a similar time to Fiona's parents, against whom Vincenzo never held a grudge. Giorgia suspended her desire for a family until Vincenzo finished grieving. To Vincenzo's surprise, Giorgia wanted to accompany him to the funeral of Fiona's father. She dressed in black and wore a veil covering much of her face.

Giorgia kept her focus on her husband's wellbeing after the deaths of Alessandro and Vittoria, who died within months of each other. Vincenzo looked upset but showed no emotion; Giorgia needed more consoling than he did. She and Sofia oversaw the endless administrative tasks associated with their deaths. Funeral planning and sorting through their belongings were the most onerous jobs they had to do. Vincenzo and Giovanni prepared the eulogy for both funeral services. They delivered their words in a calm and sobering tone, without concern for the occasion. Giorgia couldn't understand how they did it.

Giorgia started mentioning children again in the weeks after Vittoria's funeral. Almost three years since their wedding. Vincenzo would give a nod when Giorgia talked about kids, but no progress was made. They'd hardly speak to each other and certainly never go to bed together.

The death of his parents felt like another dagger to Vincenzo's heart. Two new wounds he didn't think would heal. He had a family, but it wouldn't be the same anymore. He knew he shouldn't have married Giorgia. He wished a different life for himself.

25

Camp Week

December 2022

I wanted to do the community service camp. Home each night, for a few hours of labour during the day. No cabins or tents, no teachers, and nobody keeping you up all night.

Throwing dirt from one heap to another, sorting clothes for the goodwill, or making cold calls for a Christmas appeal. I'd stay with Mum and Phil and get home earlier than I would on a school day. Afternoons and nights would be mine.

Eliot and I put each other as our preferences for the camp, both of us ticking 'customer service' as our area of interest. This would land us as a store clerk or a sales caller. Eliot ended up getting a volunteer job for a mental health charity. Branderson kept me far from it.

Too talented for something cushy, Rusty. You need a challenge. I'd be joining Branderson, the rowers, and the rest of the footy players on a four-night hike across the Shoalhaven, a winding river two hours south of Sydney. The route was so long and obscure that we were given steel hiking sticks to help us manage the terrain and needed a truck to offload our meal packs at the nearest road to our campsite each night. We'd be up before sunset and making our tents in the dark. Unless we were ahead of schedule.

These next five days will be all about finding – then destroying – our limits, Branderson said, pacing up and down the semi-circle he ordered us to form around him. *Each one of you were selected because you excel in your chosen sport. When you're hiking up a rock surface, striding through tall grass, or wading through the Shoalhaven, I want you to think about what you've done on the footy pitch, on the water, at the crease, and at the end, you'll be telling me how you can give more next year.*

The week wouldn't be very fun. The camp instructor, a man in his late twenties with five piercings on each of his earlobes, took position at the front of the pack. He would do this with a rotating cast of unenthusiastic students and overzealous teachers every week, setting the pace of a moderate jog for the rest to follow.

Branderson stayed at the tail. *Make sure no one's slacking off*, he said. He wore a dirty, sky-blue t-shirt with 'Detroit Motor Club' printed in cursive, and a dark purple hot rod below it. The shirt would come to just below his belly button. It revealed the rolls on his gut whenever he wasn't perfectly still.

He wore khaki shorts that looked to be cut from a pair of trousers, and worn-out hiking boots. Beads of sweat gathered on his temple minutes after we left the base camp. A hilly walk along the road splitting the cow paddocks, then slipping into back-burned, desolate bushland. His place at the back reflected his ability, not his authority.

During the season, Branderson would send one of his assistant coaches, usually a young PE teacher learning the ropes, on our warm-up lap of the field. He'd make the person at the back of the group sprint to the front, followed by the next person at the back, to make sure we were never slacking.

There'd be none of that this week, never mind from him. He'd be the last one to put his pack on after a water break and could hardly push out a word when we had a minute to sit down. Commands to work harder or stop slacking would be best directed to himself.

Branderson would resume his persona at nighttime. The instructor, who led us into camp each night, would have their two-man tent assembled by the time he had stopped panting. He'd tuck into the chocolate muesli bars in his meal pack and cushion his head on his fleece jumper while we built our homes for the night.

Then, the supercoach clichés would be back. *You need to demand more of yourself, Patrick. Rusty, I was on your tail all day. I don't want to see a speck of you tomorrow.* He largely lashed out at his own players. *Dig in for once in your life.*

This was how the week went. On the good days, we'd get enough light to kick a ball around before dinner. We'd get into our site, always a small clearing next to a random paddock or bushland, around 6pm, after walking over uneven rocks, up dusty hills, or through tall grass all day. I'd have energy to cook on these days. Usually a chicken stew or pasta, cooked over a travel-sized propane gas stove. The biggest challenge was finding a level spot away from the wind, made difficult by the 25 other people trying to do the exact same thing.

Only two of the Pasifikas from our team were on the hike. The other told his Housemaster he couldn't swim, even though there were photos of him surfing on his Instagram. The other two were especially unhappy to be here. They would make quips at Branderson or the Anglos from time to time but were otherwise just panting or grunting to themselves.

We never spoke to the rowers, unless to laugh at something dumb they said. They'd be given extra meals and snacks every night. *Keep them fuelled during their season*, Branderson explained to the rest of us. I was told to make up a tent for the two seat one night. Apparently, he sprained his shoulder over the weekend. I didn't hammer any of the pegs in or put a groundsheet under the tent. He'd have to hope for a perfectly still night.

Branderson was getting along famously with the rowers, who were eating up his bouts of praise. After dinner, he'd tell us about how fit we all were and what we were destined to achieve. You could see the rowers' eyes light up when the words fell off his tongue.

Won't waste a second, Mr Branderson. You got it, Sir. An understated grin would peel onto Branderson's face each time he got such a response.

Branderson cornered me when he was in a particularly chirpy mood. We were hiking through a calm pocket of the Shoalhaven; a narrow track next to a part of the river that moved more like a creek. Every now and then we would cross it, trudging through water up to our shins. For no more reason than to test us, it seemed. We walked on flats the rest of the day, using the makeshift bush track to guide us to a grass patch, where a cow and its two calves grazed by the fence. This is where we stopped for lunch.

Branderson spoke up after our third river crossing of the afternoon, forty minutes after lunch. I was getting sick of the feeble exercise and was looking forward to finishing the week. We chose to wake before sunrise the next day to get back to camp by lunchtime. This way, our instructor said, we could get some free time by the pool or do an actual camp activity before we headed home.

Rusty. I turned to face him. *Why are you lagging behind? You should be up with the rowers mate.* Branderson's stumpy forearm wrapped over my shoulder as he said it. He had a literal hold on me.

He pushed me forward after slapping my back twice and ordered me to the front of the line. The track had become narrower than the width of my shoulders, and the instructor had already told us we would slip into the river, or pull someone else in, if we tried to overtake here. I would have to wait until we stopped for water or were spat onto a clearing.

Poke, poke, poke. Branderson found another use for his walking sticks. Most of the group had tucked them to the sides of their packs, only using them when ascending a rock face or striding through tall grass. For a few minutes each day.

Work harder, Rusty. Move quicker mate. No winger should be moving that slow. What chance have you got of catching someone on the footy pitch with that sort of stride?

He was making it his mission to crack me. Even when I got to a jogging pace, he was there, poking and poking across my spine and shoulder blades. I knew I was eluding him when his sticks could only reach the small of my back. But then the person in front would slow, and he was back, poking up the sides of my neck.

Unlike the rowers, I already knew Branderson's tricks. He let all hell come down on me at half-time of my debut match in first grade. It was a trial game, against a school from Mudgee that had come down for a hit-out. I'd played a decent game so far, scoring two tries in the corner and making some strong tackles when the ball was down my side. He wasn't impressed.

What the fuck was that Leonardi? You're a fucking kid, you clearly don't belong at this level. It was a mistake to even think you could cut it here. You're a lanky, gym kid with no fucking talent.

He stormed out in a huff, a few minutes before we were due back on the field. Nothing to anyone else. All for me. Some of the Year 12s smirked when he left, others simply gave me a pat on the back. I finished the game with four tries, and we won comfortably. Branderson shook my hand once I was back in the change room. *You needed the rev-up, son. Good start. Lots to improve on.*

The siege mentality had returned, this time hundreds of kilometres from Clarendon. Branderson knew I couldn't walk any faster than the guy in front of me. He counted on it. All I could do in that moment was put up with it. Finally, a drinks break.

Pathetic Rusty, he muttered between sips of his CamelBak. *I want a much bigger effort tomorrow. This isn't a holiday, you're here to work.*

I didn't have time for water. I stood next to the instructor, who was already packed up, to make sure I was at the front of the line. I didn't want to see Branderson for the rest of the day. Let alone be within poking distance. So I stayed at the front. Even when we were scattered onto a dirt road as wide as three SUVs, I made sure I was furthest away from him.

I was the first to get into the campsite that night, so I could choose where to pitch my tent. I set up across from where our instructor had started hammering down pegs for himself and Branderson.

It was our last night in tents, so Branderson called for a team-building session around the campfire. Even though it would've been at least 25 degrees that night. He'd spent half an hour using kindling and his gas stove to get it going.

I took a seat on a carved tree trunk, which – with four identical logs – made a pentagon around the firepit. I sat next to the Pasifikas, who seemed equally over it. The rowers occupied the logs on either side of us, three of them comfortably taking up the length of each trunk. Branderson sat himself between two Anglos on a log facing us, while the instructor, uninterested, sat by himself on the other bench.

Boys. Branderson cleared his throat. *Boys. We've been through a lot this week, testing us both physically and mentally.*

You've each earned the respect of the bloke next to you over the last few days, so I want us to get a little vulnerable with each other tonight. Whether you like it or not, you're part of a brotherhood now. A brotherhood full of elite athletes with a lot of talent and experiences to share with each other.

I'll get us started. The worst was yet to come. *What I'm most scared of is failure.* He took a deep breath. *I'm petrified of not being the man I want to be, the coach I want to be, the teacher I want to be.*

That's why I push myself every day to be better, so I can push you guys to reach your potential. You blokes will be my legacy. I could see the camp instructor roll his eyes. *You're the people I wake up for every day, to push to become the best athletes you can be.*

So your success can, hopefully, be my success too. He looked to the ground and lowered his voice to almost a whisper. *And if you fail, well, I'm a failure too. And that's what keeps me up at night.* He took a long pause, then raised his head back to us.

Any questions? Good. Let's start on my right, and we'll go around from there. He turned to one of the rowers. *Let me hear it.*

One by one, the pentagon shared their greatest fears. I didn't know what I was going to say and was waiting to hear everyone else's responses to gauge my own answer. Then, it was my turn. Something came to me.

I'm most scared of not being the best version of myself on the footy pitch and letting down the people that have worked so hard for me. Whether that's Mr Branderson pushing me during the season, or even keeping me honest during the past few days, or Mr Humphries devoting his afternoons to me in the offseason, I want to be the best for them, because my success is their success. But my failure, as Mr Branderson said, is also their failure. That's what I'm most scared of.

I glanced back up for a millisecond before gesturing to the next person. The rest of the group awkwardly stared into space, equally disinterested in my answer as I was in theirs. Our leader was playing with some twigs, peeling the bark and snapping them into smaller pieces. A pile had gathered at his feet.

I'd been learning the art of bullshitting since I started at Clarendon. The camps were infamous for their cliché character-building activities.

On Year 7 orientation camp, we had to answer: 'I will be successful at this school if __ (fill in the blank)'. Year 9: 'The friend who could stop me from reaching my potential is __.'.

They started splitting the camp groups based on academic or athletic acumen in Year 10. Most people answered these questions as I did. We all had a pretty good way of getting through these sessions without actually offering much to our teachers.

Flattery was the easiest way through. Especially for Branderson. He adored us. I was hoping the Pasifikas, the only other footy guys who spoke before me, wouldn't mention him. They talked about family and culture, which gave me the perfect opportunity to come across as thoughtful, but more importantly, original.

The remaining answers contained the same garbage. But I already said it, so Branderson seemed less interested. He spent the next day pestering us to pick up our pace, even threatening to add extra sessions to our holiday gym schedules if we weren't quicker. He'd use his hiking sticks to smack those he thought weren't walking fast enough. He didn't say a word to me.

26

Archery

December 2022

We boarded the Greyhound after breakfast on Thursday morning. Our first hot meal that week that wasn't cooked on a pocket stove. We got back to the campgrounds at four o'clock on Wednesday afternoon. It was later than anticipated, but still freed some time for an actual activity.

Archery. *Fucking archery.* The one that all the other camp groups, the ones that spent their week sleeping in beds and eating food from a kitchen, didn't want to do.

We threw our packs and walking sticks by the activities hall and set out for the range. It was hidden on the downward slope of a small field about 200 metres from camp, in the same direction that we left for our hike at the start of the week. Our instructor glanced at his safety manual, then briefed us.

Three fingers pulling back. Index finger, middle finger, ring finger. Pull to your eye, keep your elbow square, stay composed, shoot. Whatever you do, don't walk between the targets and the shooting range. Not until I say so.

My first shot bounced off the hard soil five metres from the target. It attracted some cheap laughs from the group. I rested the bow on the floor and retired to the wooden picnic bench at the side of the range. Where the two Pasifikas had been since the briefing finished. We sat in silence until Branderson ordered us back. Now we sat on the bench behind the shooting area, made up of three equidistant two-by-four wooden planks. None of us took any shots. The group packed up when we started to lose sunlight. Dinner was about to be served.

Rusty! Good to see you, how'd you go mate? Patterson was always annoyingly earnest. *Mr Branderson told me he worked you boys hard. Gee, you smell like it.*

He never went on camp and would miss us by the end of the week. The House would get lonely if it was left to one person. I indulged his fist bump and walked to my room.

Something Else Unexpected

December 2022

It was called a trial separation, but there were no plans for it to be temporary.

The first domino fell through Patterson. He called me down on Thursday afternoon, a couple of hours after I returned from camp. *Oi, Rusty,* one of the other Year 10s poked his head inside my door. *Go downstairs, Patterson's after you.*

He'd never use his office outside of school hours. Knocking on your door meant you were in trouble, trapping you by the TV meant he wanted to be mates. Sometimes he'd book the pool table, or push the younger boys off it, to bond with a student he thought was struggling.

Patterson was standing by the bottom of the stairs this time, tapping his feet and playing with his fingers. *Hey mate.* He spoke softly. *Follow me.*

We walked through the corridor leading to the teachers' rooms, and slipped through the locked, sliding door leading to his office. He had one next to his classroom on campus, but this was the one given to him as housemaster. The two filing cabinets behind his desk contained medical documents and legal stuff. *All the boring things,* he would say. *For me to worry about.*

He sat down behind his desk. His eyes didn't waver from mine. *Rusty, the plan for tomorrow was for you to be picked up by your parents, right?* I nodded. *And you've started packing away all your stuff for the holidays, yes?* Yes. *Ahead of getting your new room next year.* Nod. He'd never been this stiff.

The plans have changed a little bit. Your Mum won't be able to pick you up tomorrow. You'll be able to stay Friday night in the House, but then we'll have to be out on Saturday. That's the same for everyone else in the House, even the country boys. I have to get out by Monday. He drew a breath. *There's nothing for you to worry about. I just wanted to keep you in the loop.*

Mum called me that night. She quivered when she spoke. Her tears muffled some of her words. She was soft-spoken and a little defeated. I hadn't been the first person she spoke to that day.

Phil left two days ago. *Sometime while I was at work,* Mum told me. The desk, books, and frames were already gone. Mum first thought they'd been robbed. Though she couldn't understand why the thieves hadn't touched the jewellery, TV and computers. The note tucked under the fruit bowl enlightened her.

Phil never sold his apartment in the city. He'd be back in the next couple of days, the letter read, to get more of his belongings, and would be in touch about a removalist to help with the bigger items.

Half the money from their shared account was withdrawn that morning. An official document reflecting their separation landed in her inbox in the afternoon. The email said, in simple terms, Phil wanted to get his stuff out of St Ives as soon as he could, and start afresh.

Mum thought he had come over a second time later in the week. Probably on Wednesday. He took the plastic chairs and leather couch on this visit. Must've been with a removalist, she reckoned. *No way he could've done that without help.*

She then shifted to me. *I'm not sure if I'll be able to grab you tomorrow, Rusty. Work's been so busy this week. You'll be okay to wait another night for me? Then it's two whole months away from school. One night can't make too much of a difference.* I couldn't get a word in. *You're still not allowed to just take the bus home, are you?*

No, I wasn't. That was Jock Evans' fault.

Jock was a boarder from Yass who played first grade prop for three years. He convinced his housemaster that his parents were coming down to Sydney for the first week of summer and wanted to celebrate the end of the schoolyear at a restaurant in the city. Then, he explained, they would go back to Yass for the holidays.

Jock's housemaster was woken by a cop from Killara Police Station that night, who said Jock had asked an off-duty police officer to buy a bottle of vodka for him. The cop took his money (50 bucks, so it goes), walked into the bottle shop, and called his buddies over. Jock was cornered in a back-alley behind the shops when the cop cars circled.

Housemasters were now only allowed to dismiss their students if they were being driven by a parent or boarding the Greyhound. They would have to see both happen with their own eyes to give the sign-off. Even then, they had to verify their home addresses with the coach driver to make sure there was no funny business.

The thing with Jock happened well before my time here, but the policy hadn't changed. So no, I wasn't allowed to *just* take the bus home.

The final day of the schoolyear went as I expected. The day boys floated in for the morning, then floated out in the afternoon. Gliding past the gates, into the wild. Some of the boarders, mainly from interstate or overseas, had cleared out last night or early this morning. It was just me and the country boys, who'd be scratching down the gates if it meant they could get out sooner.

The leftover meals from speech day were ferried to us for dinner. The sourdough bread rolls were served on old china with a huge Clarendon crest touching the sides of each plate. Far fancier than anything I'd seen in the dining hall. We then played touch footy on the quadrangle. We'd be shooed off by the gardeners or a stuffed-up teacher on any other night. Just us and Patterson were left.

Then Dad turned up. I looked again, to make sure my eyes weren't deceiving me. *Dad was here.* That was a surprise. He hadn't been at Clarendon since Year 7 orientation day, but he looked to be wearing the same singlet he tucked under his sauce-stained hoodie four years ago. Today, in the first week of summer, he wore the singlet, khaki work shorts, and sandals with no socks.

One of the juniors asked who he was, but I didn't say anything. He was pacing, back-and-forth, in front of the House. I hung back, and only made contact once the rest of the group filed through the dirty glass doors.

Without saying a word, he stepped forward and wrapped his arms around me. *How are you doing?* His hug was more of a clasp than a cuddle. *You're okay?* I nodded at both questions.

Your mother told me about what's going on at home. I was now wondering how he got here without suspicion from Bella. They had been married for almost two years now. I didn't think she liked me or what I represented. *Can I take you home? Your Mum told me you'd have to wait another night for her to pick you up.* Slower now, I nodded. I told him to stay where he was and give me five minutes.

First, I slipped through the sliding doors to find Patterson. I figured after yesterday's meeting, that door was now open for me. There was another small, wooden door on the other side of his office, which led to his granny flat attached to the back of the House.

Patterson was in his office, filling out some paperwork for the coach tomorrow morning. *Rusty! What's going on?* I explained that my Dad was here, and that he'd drop me off tonight. *Are you sure that's a good idea?* I reminded him that it wasn't him leaving my Mum. *That's Phil, not my Dad,* I repeated to Patterson.

Oh yes! The one with the tracksuit. Do you need help packing up?

Patterson and Dad were chumming like old friends when I stepped through the dirty glass doors. I dropped my two duffle bags to the pavement and stood in front of the two men.

Dad was dominating conversation. The thudding of my bags hitting the concrete drew his attention to me. *The big man on campus!* I didn't know what he was saying. *That's what this man tells me you are around here.*

Best footy player in the house, Patterson added. Pride was overflowing from his pupils.

Dad roared with laughter. Patterson didn't know what to do, except absorb the weight of Dad's shoulders, which jerked towards him with every howl. He couldn't comprehend Dad's disregard for it all. *Alright, you ready to go?* I nodded. *Let's go.*

Patterson reached his arm out just as we began walking up the hill. *Have a great break, Rusty.* I shook his hand and turned away.

The green BMW hatchback, fixed with the old leather bench seat, was parked in front of the Clarendon gates. If they were opened, which was only reserved for a ribbon-cutting or if someone important visited, Dad would've driven right through.

It belonged to my Zio when I lived in Leichhardt. He and Dad would sometimes drive it to a job, or to watch a football game. Nobody else would use the car, which would be covered in an oversized grey tarp at other times.

Dad bought it from him a few years ago. They still didn't use it much, he told me. *Giorgia thought it would been a good thing to have.*

An old baby seat had been chucked in the boot at some point. The fabrics on the seatbelt and corners had started to fray, and stains from mushy foods and baby formula sprayed a disgusting cream colour across the dark blue cushioning.

One of your cousins, Dad told me. He slammed the trunk door. *Came with the car.* Giorgia would've liked having a baby seat. There must've been a story there.

Dad could've had a conversation with himself. He was telling me about a jobsite he was working at in Rozelle, a couple blocks from the shipyards he spent a lot of his time at when he was younger.

A big dispute between the government and the union. *Wage caps*, he told me. *They're going mad. All the workers walked because the union told them to. Until the government agrees to a raise. We got word a couple weeks ago and have been there ever since. Long days, but no problems. There's so much work, Zio and I are doing so well.*

We turned off Mona Vale Road at St Ives half an hour after leaving Clarendon. *This area's nice eh? A street here's as wide as three back home. The trees and flowers, too. They take their gardens very seriously.*

I shrugged for a couple of seconds, then realised we were on my street. It was eerily quiet for a Friday afternoon. It was almost impossible to find space to park at this time, when most the rats would be working from home. *Packed on Mondays too*, Phil used to tell me.

Could spot at least one parked car on the street for every house, he would declare. *Wouldn't see it a couple of years ago, you'd be lucky to see one car for every three houses during the workday. COVID has changed it all.*

None were outside our place today. Dad pulled half the car onto the kerb, mounting it just in front of our garage. This was Mum's spot; the street was parked up by the time she got home from work.

The whole street was empty. I could see some of the old, dinged-up cars that had been abandoned at the end of the road. They were parked on opposite sides but were so far away that it looked like they were touching. The boats propped up by metal trailers and water-resistant cushioning must've already been dragged to the beach for Christmas. They would spend most of the year under the leafy, overhanging trees on our street. The grey, thick tarps were the only thing stopping an offshoot developing on the dinghies. It also allowed the remorseful owners to forget about their purchase for most of the year.

We parked a few steps from the front door. I knew Mum wouldn't be home. I gave Dad a hug, walked up the steps, reached under the doormat for the key, and opened the door. I could hear his BMW screech away as the lock flipped.

I instantly understood Mum's concern about the place being robbed. Phil had taken half our things, mostly the boring stuff at that, but the soul of the place, as much as I hated to admit it, had been ripped away.

Each room felt bizarrely incomplete. Like we were in between homes. My bedroom, one of Phil's pet projects, was naked. All that was left was a navy-blue mattress, held by a black foldable bed frame he used to push to the side when he once used the room as a study. Next to the kitchen, where we'd watch TV after dinner, was a single brown couch Mum had taken from Nan's place in Glebe. The living room's L-shape had become an I.

Mum's bedroom didn't change much. She still had her bed, a queen-sized mattress braced by its timber bed frame, with matching bedside tables and cupboards intact. Phil never had much of a wardrobe, and while

I assumed he had taken his clothes with him, I didn't want to inspect any further.

I opened the back doors and walked six steps to the shed. Phil had taken the plastic foldable table with him, along with the miscellaneous tools he'd kept there, and some of the free weights he had bought for me.

Even if I wanted to work out over the next two months, I thought to myself. I'm sure Branderson would still find a way to have a go at me.

Mum got home a couple of hours after I did, with a pepperoni pizza and reeking of wine. The screech of her wheels turning onto our street, about 200 metres from my bedroom, was the only reminder I was given of the outside world that night. I met her with a hug.

She marched to her room after handing me the pizza box. I spent the night in front of the TV, the 24-inch flatscreen Phil would take any day now, watching the footy and eating the lollies I'd stockpiled in my dorm over the year. It wouldn't belong to me next year, so I had no choice but to take them.

I never heard Mum come out of her room. Except for when she put the shower on after getting home. Even then I couldn't hear any footsteps passing through the corridor.

After the footy game was over, I tiptoed past the kitchen and up the stairs towards her bedroom. There were signs of life. She had left her towel soaking in a ball on the bathroom tiles, which felt like a rag when I picked it up. The toothpaste tube had been left open on the kitchen sink, and the bathroom cabinet with her nighttime medicine had been left ajar. Despite 'His' not being here anymore, she kept all her stuff on 'Her' side of the bathroom.

Footmarks led me to her bedroom, which had its door shut and lights off. I tiptoed down the stairs, walking side on to avoid any harsh cracks on the floorboards, then sidestepping through the corridor before falling onto my mattress. I realised my toothbrush was in the bathroom cabinet upstairs. Too much trouble now. I couldn't risk waking her up. She needed to rest.

I grabbed the spare pillow from the couch Phil didn't take with him and rested it on the top of my mattress. I dropped onto it – no cover sheet was needed for a summer night in December – and closed my eyes. It took me hours to fall asleep.

28

Phil and Fiona

November 2022

Fiona sensed something going awry in her marriage. She started to feel concerned months ago, when she realised that she and Phil had broken the routine that kept them on the straight and narrow as a married couple.

They used to hike through Gadigal National Park most weekends, parking by the oval before using the public bushwalk to arrive at The Cascades – a series of rock pools flowing between the natural platforms separating St Ives from Belrose. Fiona would swim in the water during summer, while Phil would climb to the highest platform for the best view.

They would shop at the farmers' market at the St Ives Showground on Saturday mornings or do some window shopping in Chatswood on a miserable day.

Fiona and Phil hadn't spent much of a weekend together for months. Fiona – a bona fide, unapologetic workaholic – always brought a report from the office to analyse over the weekend, while Phil had taken a much more devoted interest in his home projects. This included a refurbishment of Rusty's bedroom, which used to double as Phil's study when Fiona's son was at boarding school.

Fiona's concerns about her marriage were confirmed in early November, when Rusty returned home on the Thursday night after his exams finished. Her son had told her that Phil had been acting a bit strange around him lately, including asking some personal questions about himself and Fiona's life before he was around.

Fiona knew this was her fault. She owed Phil more honesty, but it was too painful to describe the life she once lived. Moving to St Ives was a move for her state of mind if nothing else. She wanted to leave everything else on the other side of the Harbour Bridge. It was her fault that Phil had brought Rusty into their personal squabbles.

Phil's eyes brightened when Rusty arrived home on the Thursday night after exams had finished. Fiona had sent him to collect Rusty at the shops, which he had obligingly done. Phil, with a perceptible spry in his voice, suggested the three of them have dinner at the St Ives Hotel that night. He and Fiona used to play trivia at this pub but hadn't been for almost a year.

Fiona was pleased with Phil's suggestion, but his enthusiasm was confronting. As much as he loved Rusty, he wasn't proposing a special dinner because of his return. Her son had always been an easy-going customer and would prefer a takeaway pizza to a sit-down meal. Phil was excited because tonight, he didn't have to share a table with just his wife.

Fiona didn't blame him; the sterility of suburbia had infected her years ago. She spent her days working, thinking about work, thinking about Rusty, or sleeping. Rarely would she accept Phil's invitations for an afternoon stroll or join him for a homemade coffee in their backyard. She would pretend to be asleep when Phil made an approach for sex, which had become increasingly scarce over the course of their relationship.

It wasn't her focus. Even when she would go on hikes or shopping with Phil, she would only do it to allow her brain to rest after another week of bookkeeping. She thought her parents, who had both died in the years after she left her first husband Vincenzo, would be proud of the life she had carved for herself.

Fiona, Phil and Rusty sat at a plastic, rectangular table at the St Ives Hotel for dinner. The table stood next to a glass windowpane separating its diners from the cars dashing across Mona Vale Road. Phil and Rusty sat closest to the windowpane, while Fiona sat next to her husband.

Phil leaned forward during the dinner, taking interest in Rusty's answers about school and rugby. He'd keep his shoulders square and head straight when Fiona spoke, hardly paying attention to what his wife had to say.

Fiona noticed but understood. She went straight to the shower after arriving home, before falling into bed. She didn't hear Phil come into the bedroom and left for work while he was still snoring.

***

Phil left Fiona on the last Tuesday of November, a few weeks after their dinner at the St Ives Hotel. He packed up some of his smaller belongings, including his set of hardback novels and fold-up desk, into his sandy-brown Sedan, bound for a new life in his old apartment in the city.

This wasn't his goodbye to the St Ives townhouse. He knew it wouldn't be that simple. He had finalised a formal separation email the previous week, which was scheduled to land in his wife's inbox at 5:00pm that afternoon. There would be several removalist trucks ordered, financial details rearranged, and legal documents signed. Phil felt overwhelmed but reassured. What he and Fiona had hadn't been a marriage for some time.

Phil had one more thing to do before he could leave. He had spent two hours the previous night writing a handwritten note to Fiona and Rusty, explaining his decision and his hopes to remain amicable in the future. In it, he shared with Fiona his gratitude for their time together and assured her that he would pay his share of Rusty's school fees until he graduated. He also enclosed a message to Rusty, thanking him for his warmth and company, and shared his hopes for them to maintain a relationship despite his separation from his mother. Phil loved Rusty as a son. He was the closest thing he would ever have to a child of his own.

The letter was addressed solely to Fiona, and tucked under the fruit bowl in the kitchen. Phil would let her decide if she wanted Rusty to see his message.

***

Fiona didn't believe it until she arrived home. The bookstand by the TV filled with crime novels and travel books was gone. Small clumps of dust that had formed under the bookstand were the only clue that something used to live there. Some heavier items, such as their TV and couch, would be taken by removalists over the next week, Fiona was informed over email. Phil had taken his fold-out desk from the shed, and the free weights he bought Rusty to help him for his rugby season.

Only once she assessed the damage to her home did Fiona begin to cry. For the first time in her life, nobody was left to look over her.

Her father Jack had been dead for almost a decade now. Heart attack. He was by the Glebe foreshore when it happened, smoking a cigarette and stealing a moment from his wife. Caroline knew what her husband was doing each time he said he was going out for a paper but didn't mind too much. She knew it was too late for him to change.

Jack was pronounced dead in the ambulance. No chance of resuscitation. Fiona didn't know what to tell Rusty, who had never dealt with death before. She told him that the doctors fought to keep Grandad alive until the bitter end, including a gruelling last-minute surgery, but that there was nothing they could do to save him. In reality, Jack's lifeless body stayed on a hospital bed for two hours, and once Fiona and Caroline said their final goodbyes, his body was trolleyed to the morgue. Fiona didn't think her son needed to know about that.

Caroline's death was far duller. Dead for a day or two, discovered by the unfortunate cleaner who would arrive at Fiona's mother's home each week to vacuum the floors, dust under the shelves and cabinets, and mop the floorboards.

The state of Caroline's death mirrored Fiona's attitude towards it. She had prepared herself for a life without parents since her father's death two years prior. Fiona was now Rusty's mother, and nothing else. She forced herself to be okay. For her son, if nothing else.

Thinking about Rusty made Fiona more upset. Jack and Caroline looked after Rusty after her separation from Vincenzo, in the weeks when Fiona didn't have the strength to be a mother. She dreaded sharing the news of another failed marriage with his son, who – to Fiona's relief – had embraced Phil since he met him. Rusty did make the occasional joke at his expense, but this was all just in good fun. She didn't know how he would take the news of their separation. She wasn't ready to tell him.

Fiona first called Rusty's Housemaster. He allowed Fiona's son to stay an extra night in the boarding house, owing to personal circumstances Fiona didn't offer much detail on.

Then Fiona's fingers dialled for Leichhardt. She didn't quite know why. The phone kept on ringing, casting doubt on her decision to call in the first place. After all, she was calling her ex-husband about her impending divorce from her current husband. Fiona was just about to press the red button when she heard Vincenzo's voice splutter through the receiver.

Vincenzo was just as surprised to hear Fiona's voice as she was about calling him in the first place. He was upset to hear about her and Phil's separation, and equally bothered about its effect on Rusty. He offered to collect his son from the boarding house on Friday afternoon, to which Fiona accepted. Vincenzo shared a moment of warmth with Fiona, then hung up.

***

Fiona was petrified of facing Rusty on the night Vincenzo dropped him home. She stayed late in the office that day, glossing over reports she would normally take home with her. These documents weren't urgent nor did they require her immediate attention. She read them over multiple glasses of wine, which she poured from a vintage Penfolds Shiraz gifted from the family-run bakery in Roseville, a longtime client. She knew that she was stalling but didn't have it in her to go home.

Fiona knew Rusty wouldn't say anything to hurt her. He was a considerate boy who had always looked after his mother. He sounded calm when she spoke to him on Thursday night, but she was worried her son was only being brave for his mother, who was sobbing throughout the phone call.

It was the look of disappointment on Rusty's face that Fiona dreaded, something he would be unable to hide when they were under the same roof. This was all she could imagine on her drive home. The wine made her tipsy, even drunk, but she felt like she could drive. She hoped there would be no random breath testing on the Pacific Highway.

In the end, she felt too overwhelmed to look her only child in the eye. She trudged through the front door of her townhouse and into the back room, following the glow from Phil's TV. Rusty was sitting on the lonely brown couch that used to belong to Fiona's parents and rose to hug his mother when she arrived by the kitchen counter.

Fiona handed a takeaway pizza to her son, who returned to his position on the brown couch. She rubbed the back of his shoulder and head with the inside of her hand, then ascended the staircase to arrive at her bedroom. She kept the lights off, dived onto the mattress, and started to sob.

29

Leichhardt

December 2022

Dad did a double-take when he saw me plonk my duffle bags on the front landing.

Raffaele, what are you doing here? Are you alright? I knew he'd be home. As he did when I was a child, he still spent his weekends lazing around the house, like a zombie waiting to be revived on Monday.

He and Zio weren't allowed to smoke at home anymore. Bella barred it once she arrived. *Second-hand smoke, kids, health issues, all that stuff,* he told me when he drove me home the previous week. He'd sneak in a drag after work, stashing the cigarettes in a locker or under some documents in his car. If he was careful, he could steal a smoke at home. But never in front of Bella or the kids.

Mum was only leaving her room every two or three days. To shower or buy groceries. I spent the first week of summer just like her, watching the hands on the clock inch closer and further away from each other. I left the house a few times, mainly to go to Clarendon to follow Branderson's draconian gym routine.

The home around me was being picked apart. I wanted to scream. Phil came over two more times during the week, collecting some of the other items he had scattered across the place. He only acknowledged me when he had to. I was in the kitchen, spreading jam on my toast when he came in to grab the wooden ornaments on the other side of the counter.

Hi Rusty. He was uneasy. *How are you and your mother going? I won't be long, just picking up some small things.* Okay. He turned to the door. *Nice to see you.*

Mum didn't leave her room. He brought a couple of removalists the second time, who helped him with a coffee table we had in front of the brown couch. Mum hid in my bedroom while it was happening. It was the only place where none of his stuff belonged anymore. Phil didn't knock or bother us.

We heard the front door close minutes after it was opened. Mum sent me out to see if Phil had left. The removalist truck was still double-parked out the front of our townhouse. Two men in high-vis were carrying Phil's bedside table, a light-coloured, wooden base with three equal-sized draw-ers. Phil had slung his dress shirts, each on a separate coat hanger, over his shoulder, all resting on his pinkie. The coffee table was already loaded in the truck, which was now in drive and ready to thud away.

Mum rose from my bed and walked back upstairs. I didn't see her un-til the next day, when I found her in the kitchen cooking eggs for break-fast.

Mum didn't want me there. She never said that, and I don't think ever would, but she had no interest in company. Being alone was her default setting. Nan and Grandad were there for me when she left Dad. She'd outsource to Sofia and Nonna when we were in Leichhardt. Now, it was just me. Granted, I needed less taking care of now than I did back then, but it wasn't like she was really here anyway.

We had never been close to Phil's family. They never approved of our home. Barry came over once after the wedding, a Christmas Eve dinner last year. He spent most of the night asking Phil what he was doing with work, and his and Mum's plans for the future. He said two things to me. *How's boarding school going?* and *Must be good to get out your Mum's hair?* I nodded and smiled at both.

I decided on Saturday that I was going to leave.

Usually, Mum and I would do something fun to start the weekend when I was on holidays. Often just a walk through the national park or getting breakfast from the showground. Sometimes with Phil. But it was quiet upstairs. She stepped out of her room at 10:30am, knocking on my door to ask if I wanted some toast. I lied, telling her I didn't feel like breakfast. I'd made myself cereal three hours ago.

I mapped out my journey on Saturday night. I would leave around 8:00am, hours before Mum would wake. Get a bus from Mona Vale Road, hop on a train at Gordon, and get a bus to Leichhardt.

I would be at Dad's around 10:00am. Sofia and Bella would be at church, which would give me some time to chat with Dad before they could get home. Hopefully, he could explain my presence when they returned.

***

Dad poured me a coffee from the rusted stainless steel coffee plunger on the dining table. It looked more decrepit than I remembered. The tablecloth must've been in the wash.

I told him everything. Phil pushing me into boarding school, moving in without much notice, all the rugby paraphernalia too. I told him about the incessant questioning over Mum's past relationships, her business, and where I fit into all of it. It was pouring out of me.

Dad was quiet through it all, shrugging aimlessly or smirking in other parts. He never really knew Phil, so perhaps he felt somewhat impartial.

He pointed me to a small, coffee-stained mattress in Nonna and Nonno's old room, who had both passed a few years after Mum and I left. We weren't invited to either of their funerals.

Gioia and Mia took my old bedroom. The same orange and blue Smith Street uniforms were tucked away in the closets at the back of the room. *For a few years*, Dad said to me.

My old mattress had been given to Mia, whose crayon drawings and finger paintings ('MIA' scratched at the bottom of each) had been sticky taped to the walls where posters of fighter planes and footballers used to be.

Nonna's room was similar to the study/bedroom Phil and I used to share. There were all sorts of miscellaneous items tucked into closets or wardrobes, with others poking from all pockets of the room. I could see cracking picture frames, old clothes, and spare linen from the doorway. What difference would two duffle bags make?

We were at the old dining table, onto our third cups of coffee, when Sofia and Bella walked in. Their eyes bulged, and their eyebrows raced up their foreheads.

The muscles around Bella's mouth tightened when she saw me. She then made a grin and came forward for a hug. Holding each of her hands were Gioia and Mia. They wore matching white sundresses. Their Sunday best.

I don't think they knew who I was. It was the 'Raffaele' buzzword that triggered their recollection, and only on Bella's prompt did they say hello.

Sofia kissed me on the cheek and asked how I was doing. She told me that Zio was out on the harbour, sailing with two old friends from the shipyards. *He'll be back tonight*, Sofia assured me.

Bella summoned Dad for an explanation once the pleasantries were over. *Vincenzo, come upstairs.* He glanced at me then stood up, taking his coffee with him. Both their footsteps went quiet at the top of the staircase. Their bedroom door shut two seconds later.

The kitchen had emptied, leaving me with the plunger and my mug. I wandered to the back landing. Gioia and Mia were running up and down the concrete beside the landing, kicking a dormant tennis ball at each other, then jumping on top of one another.

The green plastic Bunnings chairs still rested on the back landing. It was the perfect place to watch them do nothing. They noticed me, but didn't seem to care.

30

Bella

February 2019

Giorgia waved the white flag on her marriage with Vincenzo after many years of struggle. She had packed up her clothes and belongings in a bunch of suitcases and moving bags, which Vincenzo had spotted hiding in one of the wardrobes a few nights before she left. He didn't say anything, and just nodded his head when Giorgia told him.

Vincenzo spent that day resting on the green plastic chair on the back landing, smoking hand-rolled cigarettes and drinking beer. Giorgia left before saying goodbye. Vincenzo thought it was fairly civil.

The prospect of Bella excited Vincenzo. He would often see her on Norton Street, shopping for groceries or lining up for coffee. She wore pink lipstick, a tight-fitting turquoise polo, and suit pants with a laminated identification card hung by her belt loop. The emblem on her breast pocket showed the name of the Lilyfield retirement home she worked at. It was splashed on their fleet of minivans, which Vincenzo often saw ferrying their clientele from one appointment to another.

With Giorgia gone, Vincenzo did his weekly shop on Saturday afternoons. He tried the morning markets once but couldn't stand the glare of the Sicilian women roaming the schoolyards. The afternoons were peaceful and wouldn't impose on his time on the back landing each morning.

Vincenzo was queuing for coffee on Norton Street just after lunchtime when he made his move. He was just about to order when he spotted the turquoise polo enter the cafe. Bella was carrying two full bags of groceries in either hand, and was hanging a bag of grapes on her pinkie. Vincenzo ordered his long black, then asked the barista to hold his card for Bella's order. She looked too preoccupied to find her wallet.

Vincenzo felt a *tap* on his shoulder five minutes later. He was outside, resting his back on the glass shopfront window and using the back of his chair as an armrest. He'd always drink his coffee like this. Normally he'd smoke a cigarette, but he was worried this could scare Bella away. He hadn't met her yet but knew people in healthcare didn't like smokers.

She thanked him for the coffee and set his card on the plastic tabletop. Bella sat without invitation. Vincenzo was taken aback by her eyes, which were the darkest shade of brown he had seen. It complemented her olive skin, which Vincenzo knew came from Sicilian blood.

Bella's nonno had been a fisherman in Palermo before coming to Australia with his wife in the fifties. They had both since passed, but Bella still lived in their family home by Parramatta Road with her parents. Vincenzo realised he was a generation older than Bella. She looked to be in her late twenties, and he was almost fifty.

They made a habit of running into each other on a Saturday afternoon. One time they met in the morning, after Bella was forced to cover for a colleague tending to a family emergency. Vincenzo didn't mind skipping his smoke on the back landing, and hardly noticed the watchful gazes of the nonnas returning from the markets anymore.

They married about a year after their first meeting. The civil ceremony was done at a registry office in the city. Giovanni was brought as a witness, and Bella's sister, Rosa, also came along. Vincenzo thought of inviting Raffaele, but worried he wouldn't be happy with his father moving onto another marriage. He also knew that Fiona's wedding was soon, and didn't want to make it seem like he was stealing her thunder. Vincenzo always wanted to do right by her.

They opted against a big wedding; Vincenzo felt that a change of tone, after his two failed marriages, would bode well for their future. He hadn't set foot in Bar Italia for years, and had to be dragged to church, usually by Sofia, each Christmas. Both places reminded him of a time too sweet to think about now. He dreaded questions about Carlo, the joyous founder of Bar Italia who had been like family to him, and would steer clear of any talk about the Norton Street of old.

Bella moved in with Vincenzo when she became pregnant. Marriage was just a simple formality for them. She would leave her job and become a wife.

Then she became a mother. One month after the wedding. Vincenzo was apprehensive about becoming a father again but felt more assured next to Bella. Raffaele only visited on rare occasions, and for not nearly as long as Vincenzo would've liked, but Bella was always kind to him when he was there. She would slave away in the kitchen hours before he was due for lunch and wouldn't let him leave without a fifty dollar note in his pocket. It reminded Vincenzo of how his own mother was around Raffaele.

Vincenzo had always worried about Raffaele. If he would make friends, if he would finish school, if he could make a decent living one day. He didn't think he deserved answers to his questions. There were times when he would hardly speak to Raffaele when he was over. Vincenzo would spend his time on the back landing, wasting away like he had for most of his adult life. He used to only do this with his brother, but now felt no need for company. Since Bella had barred smoking in the house, Vincenzo started to drink earlier and more often.

Other times he wouldn't punish himself. He'd sit inside, and gesture Raffaele to join him in front of the TV. Sometimes his son would sit with a beer, other times a soft drink. Vincenzo would ask him about school and how Phil was treating him. He was relieved when Raffaele told him he was getting good marks. It seemed he had inherited his mother's brain.

He prayed that he and Bella's child would have a similar fate. Then they learned they'd be having children. Twins didn't concern Vincenzo as much as he thought it would. He was content working the rest of his life; he never really fathomed doing anything else.

Gioia and Mia were born on a sweltering February day, in the same hospital where Raffaele began his life. The heat didn't concern Bella, who maintained her composure throughout labour.

He hoped his new children wouldn't make Raffaele feel overlooked. He was amazed by his son's generosity; Vincenzo thought Raffaele would sacrifice his own relationship with his father if he thought it would be best for his sisters. Vincenzo still wanted to spend more time with Raffaele but didn't want to take him from his mother. He still loved Fiona very deeply, and was upset to hear about the breakdown in her marriage.

***

Raffaele found a shocked face when he dropped his bags on the front landing of his father's house. Once he realised what his son was asking, Vincenzo was ecstatic. They hadn't slept under the same roof since he started high school. He didn't know the next time he'd get more than a meal with him.

Vincenzo hardly listened to what his son was saying. He was just happy to see him in his home, wanting to be with his father. He kept his feelings to himself, and let Raffaele talk, shrugging or nodding in parts to show that he understood.

Bella needed some convincing. Vincenzo explained why his son was here, and how important it was that he stayed. He had never spoken so passionately about another person before. Bella listened, then gave her reply. They came to an agreement, and walked back to the dining table.

31

Raffaele and Bella

December 2022

Bella called me from the back landing just before lunchtime. She was sitting on the same chair I was drinking coffee at that morning. Dad was in his same seat, disinterested and embarrassed.

You'll be staying in Nonna's room, Bella explained. The one Dad showed me to that morning. *We don't think you need your own room, but you're too old to be with the girls. We'll go with that for now. But there's going to be some conditions. You're still at school?* I nodded.

You're still going to have to go while you're here, just like you would with your Mum. We're on holidays. I won't be back until the end of January. Pause.

You'll have to keep yourself busy then. Or Vincenzo will find work for you. You can't just sit around here all day. I nodded.

Your father wants you to stay for as long as you want, but we have two families here and two little kids around. We'll give you a week. Maybe we can chat in a few days, but you'll have to go back to your Mum eventually. I know what's happening. She needs you. Your father needs you to be there for her.

While you're here, you're coming to church with me and the twins every Sunday. You're going to help with the shopping, too. And if you get into any trouble, we're sending you back to your home. We don't need another child here. Okay?

With a smirk hidden beneath my smile, I gleefully nodded in Bella's direction. *Grazie, Bella. Grazie, Papa.*

Dad shot up from his seat and cracked a beer.

32

Growing up in Leichhardt

December 2022

My life here at 16 wasn't much different to when I was six. Back then, Sofia would be the one shaking me awake in the morning. She'd walk in around 7 o'clock, and wouldn't stop until I sat upright in bed.

A big jug of coffee, probably enough for two plungers, would sit in the middle of the dining table, with a few pieces of toast stacked around it. We were never allowed to drink coffee, so Sofia would spread some strawberry jam or marmalade on the toast for us. She'd be the only real adult in the house at this time of the day. Mum would be working or getting ready for work, and Dad and Zio would already be at some jobsite by breakfast time.

Nonna and Nonno would still be in bed, usually awake, but not ready to get up. I'd sometimes peek over the side of their scraped wooden door in the morning, spotting one of them staring aimlessly at the wall in front of them, while the other slept. They'd pull themselves out once we were gone, stepping down the staircase in their slippers and finishing the coffee and toast left behind. I learned this on the days I wasn't at preschool.

***

The composition of the house was different now, but the roles were similar. Bella was what Sofia used to be. She was now in charge of the kids in the mornings. I'd hear her stomp into the twins' bedroom most mornings, taking a more visceral approach to the wake-up routine.

Buongiorno, Gioia! Buongiorno, Mia! You could always hear the rhythm in it. *Time for school, andiamo!*

She would then stomp out of the room and through the corridor. Just past my room, then peeling down the staircase.

The same big coffee jug sat in the middle of the toasted white bread. I would roll out of bed once I heard Bella shut the front door. Gioia and Mia were off to preschool. Sofia was sitting at the end of the kitchen table and had started to collect the remnants of breakfast. She smiled when she saw me.

Raffaele, you remember how I used to wake you up? I returned her grin. *Sit down, I'll make you some fresh toast.*

Both her kids – my cousins – had already finished school. Leonardo, who like his father had the customary first name of Alessandro on his birth certificate, had done well for himself. He was working for one of the big banks in the city, and hadn't lived in Leichhardt since leaving for college when he was 18.

Sofia's voice softened when she spoke about her firstborn. Leonardo lived with some friends in a share house in Bondi. *Poorly kept, rotten place. How this would be if the cleaning was left to him,* Sofia smirked. *I refuse to go there.*

The other one – Luca – was just a few years older than me. He dropped out of school when he was 16.

Your Zio's son. He's at the end of his apprenticeship. Working at one of the massive high-rises at the Quay. Sofia drew a breath. *All of a sudden, he tells us he's going to live with some of his brother's friends near the city. Told us on a Thursday night, out on Saturday.*

Your Zio had been pushing them in that direction, to find their own place. It was when Giorgia was leaving, so it became just your Papa, Zio, and I.

Wasn't long until Bella came along. And for two more kids to pop out. Was just the three of us, two beds to spare. Now, more than double that.

I had never seen Sofia smoke before. It'd been reserved for the men here, a simple pleasure they could share at the end of a day's work. The women would clean the ashtrays for them, and never dream of a drag themselves.

Sofia would smoke by the back landing most mornings, sometimes on one of the Bunnings chairs. When Bella was dropping the twins off. This would be good for at least one cigarette; Bella would cut by the shops to buy some groceries or do some window shopping after the drop-off, so Sofia never felt rushed.

Tiny chunks of tobacco would be pinched from her snap lock pouch and dispersed along the base of the rolling paper. She'd lick the ends tight, press the filter around the end, and click her lighter. If this was a secret, Sofia wasn't hiding it from me. I was only going to be here for a week. She didn't care if I knew.

The nights would be like the mornings. Sofia, now the honorary Nonna of the house, would teach Bella how to cook our special Bolognese sauce around sunset. This would start on the weekends or after the twins had been dropped to school, when they'd venture out together to gather the ingredients for the sauce.

Bella would be taught which tomatoes and onions are best, and how they were meant to be cooked. She'd boil the spaghetti in the afternoon, feed it to the twins around 5, then put them down for the night.

Dad would rarely get home when Gioia and Mia were still awake. On the nights his khakis or overalls didn't stink of dirt or sweat, they reeked of beer.

Dad and Zio would always smoke when they drank. Despite their best efforts, the smell would permeate from the bottoms of their fingernails and corners of their mouths. It didn't matter though; their overshirts would be thrown in the wash that night.

Mum used to be the one putting it on the line before she went to bed. She'd try to have them dry for the next morning, but they kept a spare pair if Dad and Zio got home too late. I'd catch Bella putting these through the dryer now, sometime around 10 or 11, and grabbing them early in the morning while Dad and Zio were still asleep.

Bella kept the makeup table and mirror that Giorgia abandoned a few years ago. It was in the same corner it was always in. Her clothes were peeking out from the wardrobe doors, while Dad's – work clothes and short-sleeved dress shirts – were folded into a singular platform at the top of the wardrobe. His work boots and thongs were tucked into the floor space beneath the structure.

33

Integration

December 2022

I'd only leave the house once Bella took the twins to holiday care. When Sofia was rolling her cigarettes. I'd walk past Norton Street to get to the bus stop on Parramatta Road, or duck down to see the joggers by the bay. Both a safe distance from Smith Street.

Bella would bang on my door when I slept in, armed with the vacuum as her excuse and intimidation tactic.

Up, Raffaele, aren't you meant to be at the gym? I need to clean.

For the first few days here, I did as I was told. Which was getting to Clarendon three days a week to work myself to exhaustion.

The work doesn't stop in the holidays, Branderson would bark at us each morning. He'd come from the beach, donning a big straw Bunnings hat on his fat head, with the crumbs from his morning sausage roll balancing on his wrinkled polo collar.

Only a few others would show up. Sam recruited a couple of guys from Year 11, going into Year 12, who had played in the lower grades last season. *Easy fodder,* one of the first grade Anglos chuckled to the rest of us.

Sam would meet us at the bottom of the hill when the rowers were using the equipment. *Hill sprints today boys. Or until the rowers go back to the ergs.* He wouldn't let us put our bags in the change room. *Drop your shit here, Rusty, we can grab it later.*

The rowers were equally cocky during the holidays. They were living in the boarding houses for a holiday camp running until Christmas. Patterson volunteered as a supervisor. He would've been all too happy to spend more time at school.

A privilege, he would call it. *To do my bit for the program.* They'd be returned to their unloving parents for the two weeks after Christmas and be back inside the gates until March. Spare dorms would be made for them, while they'd spend their days working and spewing next to a stupid rowing machine.

I didn't tell anyone at Clarendon I was living with my Dad. I was worried some of them would notice me get off a different bus, or that I wasn't bringing my Clarendon Rugby water bottle to the gym with me. It was a mandated part of our gym equipment.

I gave them too much credit. Plus, as I reasoned with myself, I was a boarder. They wouldn't have considered the possibility I had a home outside Clarendon. Or that Patterson wasn't my dad, and that the boarders weren't my family.

I stopped going to these sessions after the first week. Hill sprints and lifting, it was the same shit we were doing last term. Just with some amateurs, making me look better than I was. I hadn't touched a footy since our touch game on the quadrangle.

I'd tell them I was on holiday with my family if they asked about me. They never would.

But I needed to stay out of Bella's sight. So I left home each morning at the same time, just after she had started the preschool run, and would only nip in for a really good reason. Like money for the bus, or lunch.

Dad showed me where he kept extra cash the morning I showed up at his door. It was in a small closet next to the laundry, hidden under a cream-coloured, wooden plank false bottom.

Wrap your index finger around the back – there's enough room for one finger – and flick the plank back up. Whenever you need some money, especially if I'm at work, just grab something from here. Don't tell Bella.

I'd never abuse it. Tens or twenties at a time. Bella would get suspicious if she saw me with anything else. She mightn't have known about Dad's money stash. She would never have any reason to look for a false bottom in a random cabinet next to the laundry. Bella would only go to the laundry to throw clothes into the washer or dryer, or to grab the vacuum.

She'd lounge around between drop-offs and pick-ups, watching The Morning Show and flicking through fashion magazines held for her at the Leichhardt newsagency. She'd see out the afternoons with a Zumba class and a load of washing. She was incensed the time I found her lounging on the couch, flicking through Elle with a glass of Fanta in her hand.

Raffaele! What are you doing? Go to your room or get out. Now! I had gone to training that morning but was sent home at lunchtime because I was cramping. *More of the same shit anyway,* Sam told me. *Not like you're fighting for your spot. Go home – I'll tell Mr Branderson you're carrying a knock.*

Bella was like the older, bratty sister I never had. But she actually had some influence on Dad, which meant she had some power over me. So I followed her rules, only coming back when I knew Dad and Zio were on their way home too.

***

I started most my days at the bay, before venturing up to Norton Street. It wasn't how I remembered it as a child: the Italian Forum, pizza bars with parking out-front, even the accordions that would play outside the grocers on the weekend. What replaced it was far more trite. Low-storey, high-density apartment complexes peering over their prey.

Church seemed to be more of a novelty now. A charm of this once proud Catholic village. The church bells tolled on a Sunday morning at 10am, but there would rarely be any response. I suspected much of the congregation from when I was a child, or the ones that showed up to my parents' wedding, had died in the last 10 years, or were awaiting death in some stale nursing home.

Their kids, the children of migrants, had no reason to stay in Leichhardt. They were the first ones to go to uni, get a degree, meet an Anglo – worst yet a Greek – and have kids. Somewhere else. Five Dock, Killara, St Ives. Not Leichhardt. A place they didn't have to share with their whole families, with a grassy backyard for their kids to play in.

The soul had been removed from Leichhardt. So developers swooped. They built up. And up, and up. And sideways, if they could. The detached homes with narrow concrete landings were split into townhouses and terrace homes, cut down the middle by a quick-thinking property agent. Double your money for half the work.

Heritage and culture were out of fashion. Money was in. I started a headcount of every shop I could remember from when I was a kid. Just to know what was sacred. Next, the houses I could recall. The ones with the sandstone steps leading to the balcony, protected by rusted, wire fencing at the gate. Then, the 'For Lease' or 'For Rent' signs around Norton Street. I would lose count after 20.

Cafe Gioia was still there. People would pull into the front carpark, no more than six or seven spaces, to grab a pizza through the afternoon and into the night. A lot just for pick up, but they still managed a decent crowd most nights.

Bar Italia felt like the final frontier of Italian-ness on Norton Street. The place where the charm extended beyond novelty. That's not to say it didn't cater for Australians either. They were pulling out Hawaiians from their woodfire oven, and VBs from their fridges. Tables were requested by the wall. Next to Al Pacino or Andrea Bocelli. *Next to my little friends, you know?*

Perhaps it was my nostalgia, but it didn't feel like it was when I was young. Maybe it was the new generation, who had introduced less rigid ideas of Italian culture to the restaurant. They grew up and worked with Anglos, and certainly weren't as parochial as the first Sicilians here were.

I popped in one weekday, thinking someone might recognise me from when I was young. *Anywhere you'd like to be seated?* The waitress got right to the point. I blankly shook my head. *Okay, just go wherever, I'll leave it up to you.*

I wondered if they would recognise Mum. And if they did, how they would greet her. I can't imagine Sofia or Nonna would've given positive reports of her sudden exit, along with me by her side, when they were here after church each Sunday. Giorgia and Bella taught me how fickle Italian women can be. I can only imagine the wild gesticulations that would've been made at the markets, after church, even from Mum's old colleagues down the road.

I got my gelato from the same woman that served me as a child. She would greet Mum with a hug by the door, then reach down to squeeze my cheek for just a second. She'd wear a long, black apron with pinstripes down her front. Jeans and sandshoes, and a stained, grey t-shirt poking from the sides of her apron.

She didn't look much different today. Streaks of grey hair were tucked behind her ears, and she now had a black tee camouflaging her apron. She rushed behind the gelato bar when she laid eyes on me, standing over the glass panels, inspecting what was in front of me.

What can I get you mate? Two scoops, strawberry gelato. *Alright, there you go. Have a good one.*

I'd try to get off Norton Street before the kids were let out from their holiday camps or summer jobs. Most times I'd walk along the foreshore after lunch. I thought about jogging, but this meant I would have to sneak through the house to grab my runners. I'd watch the boats glide by in the afternoons, and the children balancing rocks on the small strip of sand between the grass and water.

I found a little nook under an old oak tree hidden behind one of the rowing clubs. It was the only part of the foreshore with any substantial shade. Kids came here every morning and every afternoon; the half-hour stretch when one of their parents could log off work, or when the grandparents had mustered enough energy to deal with them.

They started to notice me on the hill at each end of the day. The parents and grandparents would offer a smile. The kids would look bemused.

I'd waddle back up the hill, returning home at five or six o'clock. It'd still be light by then, but Bella would be busy getting the twins ready for bed. Sofia would cook on these nights. I'd lie down in my room or slump by the kitchen table, basking in the last minutes of sunlight filtering through the window panels overlooking the narrow back landing. You could see the sun dip below our cracked cement wall, and the sky gradually turn to darkness.

Dad wouldn't say much when he got home, apart from a quick nod or wave in my direction. I'd click my bedside lamp off at nine or ten, and leave my room at eight or nine the next morning. And again. And again.

34

Growing up on Norton Street

July 1986

Vincenzo only really discovered Norton Street when he was 16. It was a cold night in July, when he couldn't get a wink of sleep. School was difficult, and decades of hard labouring were on the horizon. He decided to go on an adventure.

Vincenzo slowly peeled the doona from his body and inched out of bed. He was worried he would wake his mother Vittoria, who slept lightly and for short hours, and was concerned his father was already out of bed and preparing for work. He held his sandals by their straps, his index fingers curling around each shoe.

At first, he headed for the water. Down past the APIA Club. It was so cold his bones could feel a chill. It looked to be 1 or 2 in the morning – too late to be out, but too early to be going to work. The trodden dinghies and sailboats in the bay swayed to the gentle rhythm of the sea currents below. The moon lit up each boat as if it were daytime.

Vincenzo decided to change course. He could hear a bubbling noise past his house, closer to the homes near the bus stop. He shot through the narrow streets and footpaths to inch closer. It was music, then laughter, chatter, then music. It was Norton Street, the only speck of light with any signs of life attached to it.

Vincenzo had never been here at night before. It was unrecognisable. Bars and restaurants flowed down the strip, which Vincenzo knew best for its cafes and video stores. The noise ran all the way up to the Water Board depot by Parramatta Road. It housed a few brick-and-mortar buildings, all different sizes. An older gentleman dressed in a long-sleeved button-up and a woollen old man cap caught Vincenzo staring at the building.

Acqua. His bravado snatched Vincenzo's attention. *So we can drink, shower, water our plants. So we can live!.* He finished with a roar.

Vincenzo counted a dozen places pouring wine to anyone with interest, serving pizza the size of a small tyre, or with teams of baristas rushing coffee cups into customers' hands.

But it all built to Bar Italia. The music and chatter bled from the back garden and the inside tables to the footpath, where men, unable to find a seat, would be relegated to the steps of the neighbouring grocery store, which had been closed since the afternoon. They would drink white wine from the bottle, waiting to get a glimpse of the action.

Vincenzo snuck in through the side entrance. Where customers would normally enter for gelato. He couldn't find an empty seat, nor one person without a shirt or tie on. Some wore loose-fitting suits with straw fedoras or caps, which had been perched on the clothes rack or corner of their tables. Others wore white shirts and khaki pants. The women wore gowns that wrapped around their shoulders and flowed to their shins, most with dark-coloured jumpers or cardigans draped around their backs and necks.

The commotion was coming from the garden. Vincenzo could see some jerky movements and clapping at the front. The dance moves were almost as loud as the music. He inched closer, embarrassed about wearing sandals and a stained overshirt in a crowd of well-dressed people.

Black-and-white photographs of bustling cobblestone streets and arid plains with orange trees and old cottages stretched the length of the restaurant. Some of the photos had small inserts in the corners. *Messina, Palermo, Calabria, Spadafora.*

Vincenzo found where the noise was coming from after passing *Catania.* A dapper man in his forties was perched next to the glass table at the top of the patio, playing a string of harmonies and melodies from his accordion. Next to him was Carlo; the Sicilian man who created Bar Italia. He wore a loose-fitting yellow button-up, khaki shorts and thongs. The few hairs left on his dome were covered by an old man cap, which was in a dark yellow tweed pattern.

Carlo would affectionately squeeze Vincenzo's cheek every time he came into the restaurant. Always charming but somewhat reserved. Tonight, he was the ringleader. His arms pushed up and down with the music, almost like a conductor leading his orchestra.

Carlo would only place his beer down to groove with the crowd, who were all dressed to the nines. The patio had been cleared of furniture to make way for them. Tonight, it was for singing, drinking, and dancing.

A beautiful young woman stood out among the crowd. She had brown eyes and olive skin, and was adorned in a silk white dress flowing from her collarbones to her ankles. She had pushed the front of her veil over the back of her brown hair, tucking the sides behind her ears and letting the ends fall down her back. She was held by her groom, a dark-haired man in his early thirties. They were beginning some sort of ballroom dance when Vincenzo caught sight of them. It then devolved into more of a drunken, side-to-side sway.

Carlo stepped down from next to the glass table and reached for the hand of the bride, who had been catching her breath on the edge of the patio. She instantly smiled when she realised who it was. Carlo led her to the middle of the floor, the same space where she and her new husband were waltzing minutes prior, for a slow dance. He botched every move until he trod back up the patio, next to the accordion. It didn't tarnish his grin. The bride, a tad confused, looked over her shoulder for Carlo. A better-dressed old man held her for the rest of the song.

Vincenzo kept to the corner of the pavement, one foot in the patio and the other in the restaurant. Feeling embarrassed, he scurried back down the corridor of the restaurant and was spat back onto Norton Street. He could feel the footpath vibrating. The accordion blared onto the pavement, which started to blend with music from closer to Parramatta Road. Hordes of men in suits and shirts walked up and down, in and out of bars and cafes. The night looked to be at its final stanza by now.

35

Andrea

December 2022

Gioia's stomping woke me up. Only her dress shoes, the ones with the inserts giving her an oomph when she ran, could make that noise.

Mia, chop chop. Bella must've already fed them, which meant they were on their way to day care. 8:04, my phone read. As always, I'd wait until I could hear the front gate shut before making any sudden movements. I heard Mia thud through the corridor minutes later. The same shoes they bought for Gioia. The front door opened, closed, then the front gate did the same. I threw off my top sheet and twisted the doorknob.

It was another sweltering summer's day. The sun was beaming onto the concrete and gravel streets, rusting the old-fashioned steel of the cars perched on the footpaths. Too sticky to stay inside, but too hot to be outside. A good day to be at school. They'd let us take our ties off on days above 30 degrees at Clarendon, and the classrooms and gym were always air-conditioned. As was the House.

The rubber on my thongs felt like they were going to melt. I decided to go to the bay. The adjacent hill was covered with cars; they had already been plonked in front of driveways, piled into decaying garages, or stashed in dead-end turning circles. Some cars had been parked in, their drivers undeterred by overzealous rangers and grumpy neighbours. Others bled onto the park by the foreshore. This would've followed a series of aimless shuffling through the car park at Le Montage, the venue where the APIA Club used to be.

The chaos on the narrow suburban roads was mirrored by the bay. Swimming was generally frowned upon on this inlet of the Parramatta River, but there seemed to be a moral exception today. Those with boats, mainly small dinghies or canoes, would venture into the river, splashing themselves to wash the beads of sweat falling from the side of their heads.

The less fortunate ones made camp under the outgrown eucalyptus trees on the ends of the football fields. Parents would sit under their gazebos, coloured in a striped or dotted pattern, steadily erasing the beers and wine bottles in their esky.

The kids didn't want to watch the grass grow. Most gathered by the foreshore, balancing on the buffer between the rocks and the pavement. Others would be in the water. It was dirty and unhygienic, but they didn't care. Some of the older ones, one or two years younger than me, tiptoed across the narrow strip of sand between the marina and Iron Cove Bridge, looking for any unlocked canoes they could take out. Most had already been yanked out of the metal coiling sealing it to the sandstone rocks by now. It left the row of canoes, usually a dull mix of yellow, green, and dark orange, looking bare. The only chance they'd have of getting onto the water was by diving into it.

I headed for Norton Street. It was quieter on hot days. Some families had set up picnic mats under the shade sails by the park near where Mum used to work, while a group of women in their early twenties poured homemade cocktails under the big eucalyptus tree.

Others paired an iced coffee or breakfast roll with their weekly shop. They all moved at a dawdling pace. Some mothers had dropped their kids off at day care or the bay, wandering into the pharmacy to replenish their prescriptions for the week. Others sat at the tables leaking from the cafes until the sun's glare became unbearable.

The pub on the corner – the only place with a reliable air conditioner – wouldn't be open until lunchtime. I pressed my face against the glass window, cupping my hands over my eyes to see inside. It was empty. Just some chairs stacked on top of tables and beer-stained schooner glasses lying sideways on the bar. I didn't move for a few minutes, pressing my cheeks and forehead to absorb the cool from each windowpane. I only stopped after seeing the smudges and breath marks I had made. I turned my shoulder sheepishly and kept on walking.

I peered into Bar Italia. It had been open since the early morning and was the only place with a steady set of diners. They had opened the sliding doors in the front and spread five different pedestal fans across the restaurant. The back doors leading to the patio – which acted more as a wall than an entry point most the time – were also open. They made it as cool as possible. Tables were fixed along the back garden, but no one was brave enough to sit there. It was much cooler inside. I could feel another bead of sweat fall from my underarm.

The same woman, the one with the grey hairs who scooped my gelato the other day, was the only waitress on the floor that morning. She had a thick white tea towel hanging over her right shoulder, which she used to wipe the sweat off her face and neck. She ducked behind the counter after seeing me, and turned away to glide the towel across her forehead. She threw it beside the register and approached.

What can I do for you mate. Bathroom? Yep, just down the back there and to the right. I'll get you a table in the meantime.

I only realised how disgusting I was after entering the restaurant. I could see the sweat stains from each of my arm pits, and feel the moisture on my hairline and eyebrows.

I paced past the frames of Alessandro Del Piero and Andrea Bocelli, and turned from the corridor just before the back patio. I could see the staff room, which meant I had to turn to my right and push to open the bathroom. I splashed some water on my face and pits, and reconsidered ordering a coffee.

I pushed down the handle on the bathroom door and came head on with a familiar face. It was Carlo, the founder of Bar Italia who was at Mum and Dad's wedding. He was standing next to two other men, one in overalls and a stained white shirt, and the other in a short-sleeved button-up that puffed his chest hair out of his shirt. The photo was in black and white, but Carlo's shirt looked to be in a bright colour.

His arms were gesticulating above his shoulders, his mouth pinched, while mischief glowed from his pupils. The two mystery men were facing Carlo, grinning at some clever line he looked to have cracked. I could make out the wooden fencing from the back patio behind them, and some other men on the edge of the chipped wooden frame, facing away from the camera.

Carlo was the best-looking person in the shot. Over his loose-fitting shirt were a pair of dark suspenders, which attached at either side of his waist and wrapped over his shoulders. Two ballpoint pens and a notepad fitted perfectly into his breast pocket, with the lids of the pens gripped on the outsides of the pocket. A wide, herringbone tie drooped from the top of his torso, down his body and out of the frame.

His top button was undone, and the ends of his shirt had been peeled to his forearms. He sported a grey fedora. I could see a healthy head of hair on each of his sides.

The one in the middle is Carlo. He set up this whole place.

The lady with the grey hair must've noticed me lingering in the corridor. She was standing next to me, acting as the mediator between my naked eye and the wall.

I don't know who the other guys were. Guess they were close. I hadn't said a word. *This was the night of Bar Italia's 10th anniversary. Or fifth, I'm not too sure. I wasn't around back then.*

She led me into the backroom, which contained filing cabinets and loose papers stacked on another table, identical to the ones on the patio.

She took me through all the archive photos of Bar Italia. There were ones of Carlo and his wife, with two small children in front of them, outside the shopfront in the first months of the place being open. It looked almost empty; I could only count three or four large tables, with six or seven wooden chairs around each.

We wanted families, large groups to come. They'd order lots of food and wine. Especially the groups of men. Keep us in a job. She spoke so softly. *Celebrations, but also walk-ins, meetings, whatever. Then, Carlo was able to branch out a little bit.* Again, she drew for breath.

His nephews and nieces were getting engaged. Needed a place for the reception. He turned the back area, a heap of nothingness when he bought the place, into a proper party spot.

He got rid of the big tables from those photos, and put in square ones. He could squeeze up to eight or nine different groups on a summer's day. Not one like today, it would be too hot. Maybe a Sunday in November or early December. They would always be popular.

She told me how Carlo would do weddings. Stacking the tables in a back corner or storeroom, opening the patio just for dancing. He'd ask one of his sons to play the accordion. An easy rhythm, something to move to. A smile appeared on her face.

One time, when I was young, he pulled me from my table into the middle of the patio, and spun me around and flipped me through the air. He flung me onto his shoulders, and the crowd of bridesmaids and groomsmen started to dance all around us.

That was on my cousins' wedding day. He was wearing a light-blue, collared shirt with loose-fitting chino pants. Joy flowed from her pupils. *A real character.* I asked some other questions. *Dead for some time. Ten, 15 years? I'm not too sure, I would've been in my twenties or thirties.*

I spoke to Andrea for over an hour. At the back of the restaurant, with hardly any air flow to save us from the heat. Her parents came over with Carlo, from a small village ruined after World War II. After a bit of to-ing and fro-ing, they settled on Norton Street and were determined to make it their home.

He got my Papa on board, Andrea recalled. *He started life here as a fisherman, but wanted to do anything but fish.* Her smile returned.

Mum would sometimes walk me here after school and let me help until she had finished dinner. Delivering dishes to tables, cleaning up, lighting the candles or ironing the tablecloths for special nights.

Carlo was introduced to me as my Zio, despite being as old as my Nonno. He'd scoop me a cup of strawberry or raspberry gelato before I'd leave each night. He would always be at the register when I arrived after school, pinching my cheek or hurrying me to get ready.

I asked Andrea if she remembered Mum. A fair woman in her twenties with a small boy by her side. She'd come in for gelato with her son and was greeted with a kiss from the waitstaff behind the counter. We had moved from the desk by the filing cabinets to the frayed leather chairs in the other corner of the backroom. She paused, then spoke.

She would've been a similar age to me. Married into another Sicilian family. Hadn't been here for years though. She pulled herself out of her trance. *Fiona was her name.* I nodded. She pulled out more old photographs, stashed in a yellow folder. Full of Andrea, as a little girl.

After flicking aimlessly for a couple of pages, she stopped on one with a long, skinny man in a grey suit, with slicked-back dark hair and a turquoise tie ending at his belt buckle.

My Papa, Andrea said. *Him and Carlo were pretty close. He ended up looking after Carlo's finances, making sure the books were okay. Fiona came in a couple times to help. She'd straighten things out when my father needed a second pair of eyes.* I never knew that.

It was almost lunchtime. Andrea thrust up from her seat and rushed out of the backroom. *Have to get the place ready for when it cools down. People come in for pizza after a day on the water. I'll grab you a Coke, and then you can come up for gelato if you want. Call out for me.* I nodded back at her. *Lovely meeting you, Raffaele.*

I stayed in the backroom, flicking through the photos Andrea showed me. She told me to put the folders back into the filing cabinets once I was done. I took my time. All of Andrea's life was seemingly documented in these photos. She'd never been married, despite her father's best efforts. *Very old-fashioned man,* she explained. *Never understood why I didn't want his life.*

Suitors would pop up at their home, a small, detached house two blocks from the restaurant, every now and then. Her parents would organise them with other families from church. Doctors, lawyers, accountants. Labourers too. *Some incredibly handsome.* Andrea didn't pull her punches. *My parents would've married them if they could.*

Andrea never cared for the men but was always polite. She knew what being a wife would mean. *Washing down in the morning, taking kids to school, cleaning and cooking, picking kids up from school, preparing dinner for the absent husband, then putting the washing up before going to bed.* She seemed to have mapped it all out. *And the same the next day. And again. And again, and again.* She went on.

My Mamma's life. She seemed very happy. Andrea's eyes turned to catch mine. *That's what terrified me. Happy being the stereotype, without any sort of resistance. And with nothing to show for it. Some of the men, my old suitors, now come to the restaurant with their families. We act like we don't know each other, not that we really do anyway. I'd rather be lonely than not in control of my life.*

I tucked the photos back into the filing cabinet and closed the door behind me.

36

The Landing of Silence

December 2022

Dad was sitting on his plastic chair at the top of the back landing when I returned home. He had his work shirt wrapped over his neck and his steel-cap boots unlaced and dangling off each of his heels. The seawater had grouped his chest hairs into swirls from his Adam's Apple to breasts, making a spotted, rolling pattern across his upper torso.

Raffaele, good day? You been to the bay yet? It's beautiful. He must've gone down after work, joining the kids by the sand looking for something fun to do. Or maybe one of his friends on the jobsite had a dinghy they took onto the river. A lot them had small boats docked by the bay. *For fishing or just to cruise.* His shirt and boots looked dry. Probably just a swim.

I was almost run over by Gioia, who was being chased around the kitchen by her sister. They had to move the day care activities to the one air-conditioned room in the school that day. Bella wasn't happy.

Movies, all day. As if they couldn't do that here. I don't know how I'm going to get them to bed tonight. She let out a huff and returned to the boiling water on the stove. I fell onto my mattress, which had absorbed the heat from the sun all day. It felt like a furnace on my back. I pulled the blinds down, something I should've done that morning.

***

Dad must've known Carlo quite well. Probably even Andrea's dad. Nonna and Nonno knew him from Sicily. Mum knew Andrea. That means Zio, Sofia, even Bella would've been close with Carlo sometime in their lives. I asked him at dinner. *Dad, were you friends with Carlo? From Bar Italia?*

Dad turned to Zio the moment the question escaped my tongue, and started talking shop. In Italian. He never talked about work at home. Let alone in front of his family. This was reserved for the pub or the jobsite. Maybe by the back landing, with a beer in hand. Never at dinner. Dad had never seemed so reticent to a question as he did to mine about Bar Italia.

Bella butted in, frustrated about being excluded. *What are we going to do about this day care place, Vincenzo? They sit the kids down all day with nothing to do if the sun's out. It's December. What are we paying them for?*

I jerked to my side, pinching my grin with a cough that hid my face from view. Sofia's eyes also lit up, but she was more subtle than me. She also saw the irony in her question. Bella spent her days wandering around the house and taking Zumba classes. The twins would get more value watching Finding Nemo than being with their mother.

Sofia had taken Bella under her wing since she moved in. Mum never took to Sofia's jobs; she was too busy with her own work, and Giorgia wouldn't have taken any advice from Sofia. But Bella was hopeless. She didn't care for any of the things Sofia knew she was meant to care about. Like spoiling her kids and husband. It created some tension between the two.

They'd keep their distance in the mornings. Sofia wouldn't help Bella prepare her children for school or make their lunches. It was easier for Sofia with Mum. Their children were closer in age, so it was easier to click, simply through that layer of commonality.

Dad continued to stall. *Let's take another look after Christmas, okay? You're having fun there, right girls? You don't want to be at home with your mother all day, do you?* Neither of them gave much of a response. That didn't bother Dad, who had turned back to Bella by this point. *They love it! We'll just see how they go. They'll be back at school soon.*

With that, Dad was up. He'd twirled each strand of spaghetti when he spoke and would eat when Bella returned serve. He gripped the top of the chairs on either side of him to launch his escape. The fridge swung open, then shut with a thud. To the back landing he went. The Bunnings chair bulged, the bottle cracked, and he rested. Zio joined him a couple of minutes later, then Sofia helped Bella clear the table.

I sat a little longer after everyone had left, stunned by Dad's evasion of my question. I was using the spare plastic chair that usually sat on the corner of the front landing by the street. The dark green paint job had been damaged by years of exposure to the sun. It would beat down on the brick-and-mortar each morning, only to hide behind the roof after lunchtime.

Dad and Zio weren't talking much. Little grunts, or a muted laugh or shrug was the most I could make out. Their wives did something similar. They washed in silence, only communicating through body movements or hand gestures, indicating what was to be done.

There was a routine. Bella would gather the big dishes and cooking utensils (pots, pans, and strainers) from the table or stove and stack them on the counter next to the sink. Sofia would be by the sink with her washing gloves on. She'd scrub each dish that came her way, spreading the detergent and washing soap over each pot and pan to not waste a drop. She'd pull each of the dishes across her body and onto the drying rack. This is where Bella would now be, tea towel in hand and ready to dry.

Sofia wouldn't stick around to see Bella dry; she'd disappear to her room or the front landing. Dad and Zio were left on their own. Bella would shower and get the twins ready for bed once she finished drying.

I walked up to my bedroom. Each member of the house had retired to their personal quarters, which felt like an open hint for me to do the same. My mattress had become a little cooler by now.

I wondered how Mum was doing. There didn't seem to be much interest or acknowledgement of her around here. I suppose it was the elephant in the room, which I was the personification of. I only made the awkward point harder to ignore.

I hoped she was better. And had stopped crying. She seemed indifferent about me leaving. 'Okay' was the only response I received when I texted her the day I left for Dad's place. I wondered how she was feeling about it now. She'd spent her whole life with someone looking over her shoulder. Now it was just her. I hoped she was doing alright.

37

When Rusty left St Ives

December 2022

Fiona was fast asleep when Rusty left St Ives. She had spent the week after Phil left – Rusty's first week of summer holidays – in bed, lying beneath her covers and wiping tears from her eyes. She had hardly seen her son.

Fiona would only change out of her pyjamas to pick up groceries, which she replaced three times across the week. She wouldn't bother changing clothes on other days, when taking a shower was the height of her daily activity. Rusty was out most days, she figured, playing AFL at the oval or working out at his school gym.

Fiona wanted to spend time with her son, but she was broken. It killed her that, once again, the despair of a failed relationship obstructed her ability to be a mother – the one responsibility she always wanted to keep sacred.

A grocery run was required on Sunday morning. Rusty had depleted the pantry of two strawberry jam jars, both of which Fiona had bought with Phil at the Saturday markets at the showground. He would make himself four pieces of toast each morning, with a thin spread of butter separating the blobs of jam from each slice of white bread.

Fiona asked her son the previous morning if he had wanted toast for breakfast. She could replenish the jam jars from the farmers markets, which she would arrive at just before they closed for the day. Rusty surprised his mother, saying that he didn't feel like breakfast. Fiona returned to her bedroom and continued to wallow.

Rusty wasn't home when Fiona stepped in the kitchen on Sunday morning. She only suspected something unusual when she stole a glance at her son's bedroom. The duffle bags Rusty had taken from his room at Clarendon, stuffed with his clothes, schoolbooks, toiletries and sports equipment, had vanished. They had been sprawled in opposite corners of his room, torn apart after searching for items at the bottom of each bag. It left a huge mess on the floor. The closets had been emptied, and the bed was perfectly made.

Fiona returned to the back room, and reached for the thin, wooden drawer in the TV stand. She had hidden her phone there since Phil's visit a few days earlier in the week. It would be the last for the foreseeable future. She didn't want to communicate with anyone unless she was legally obligated to.

Except for her son. Who, sure enough, had sent her a message earlier that morning. Rusty was going to live with his father for a little while. He hoped to be there for at least a week.

Fiona drew a sharp breath that smacked the bottom of her lungs. The message struck her like a knockout blow. But another part of her understood Rusty's decision. He hadn't been living in a home for the past week. Fiona wasn't ready to be Rusty's mother again for some time yet. There were mothers in Vincenzo's home; ones who had no other objective but to care for their children. Her son would be happy there.

Fiona dropped her phone at the end of the drawer and pushed it back into the TV stand. She left the back room, ascended the staircase, and returned to her bedroom. The curtains were drawn, and the lights switched off. She crawled back into bed and stared at the ceiling.

For the first time in her life, Fiona was completely alone. Her son – the constant during her marriage breakdowns and the deaths of her parents – had left. She turned to her side, and tried to fall asleep as quickly as she could. Her strawberry jam supply had become the least of her worries.

38

Hands, Eye, Smell

December 2022

I beat Sofia and Bella out of bed on Saturday. The markets were on.

There was no toast or coffee on the dining table, and their house shoes – small, rubber-enclosed shoes you'd get for $15 at K-Mart – were still tucked by their bedroom doors.

The Leichhardt streets exuded a hushed excitement. As if it were pleased about a reprieve from the stomps of the work boots and dress shoes it would endure Monday to Friday. There wasn't a park on the entire street. The station wagons and sedans were mounted to the side of the kerb, making just enough room for an oncoming car to get by.

It was sunny but not too hot; the days before Christmas where you could get away with wearing a hoodie at the end of each day. From January 1st, you'd be hard-pressed to keep a t-shirt on after 10 o'clock.

Most of the food stalls were setting up when I arrived. The local merchants, some wearing Santa hats today, were preparing their used clothes or charming crockery sets further down the schoolyard.

This wasn't too much work for them; they'd stack their gear in a big cardboard box with some bed linen for protection, fold their plastic trestle table into the back of their car, and rustle up the gazebo from their sheds or front landings. Done in 20 minutes, I reckon. They'd drive their cars through the schoolyard, park at half past seven, and log their first sale a few minutes before eight. The markets began a bit later than it used to.

Each of the vendors leaned towards me, sniffing around for business. *Morning mate. Interested in this by chance?* I'd tilt my head with a smile, offering a quick nod in response. I had a $50 note that Dad gave me a few days ago, but had no plans to blow it on an antique Australiana cutlery set.

I could hear Bella's reaction already. *What am I meant to do with a bunch of teaspoons in the shape of a snake, petrify the girls?* And then there'd be the head shakes. From side to side to side. *And the 'THAT'S NOT A KNIFE' steak knives? What good's this to us?.*

We had the same cutlery now as when Mum lived with us. A wedding present for Sofia and Zio. All those years back. From a distant relative whose name wasn't worth mentioning. It was a stainless-steel set, with gold-coloured streaks down the edges of each handle. I had never seen new utensils added to the cabinet.

I strolled to the end of the schoolyard and sat on the lunch bench next to the garden bed. The grocers on the other end were rotating their best produce to the front of the stands, and keeping the bruised ones hidden from view. Just the final touches.

I walked past the barbecues, which had only just been fired up, and towards the grocers. Some stalls had two rows that snaked through a vacant corridor. It pushed shoppers through one corner, down a row, then into the next one, before spurting them out after swiping their card at the register.

The biggest stall was dedicated to Bolognese sauce. Buckets of plum tomatoes were stacked in pallets at an 100° angle, putting each one perfectly on show. Then came the onions, showcased in a similar fashion, the oregano, basil, even some chillis and ground beef, stacked in a glass mini fridge at the back. Thin, straw awnings were hung above the fruit and veg, stopping them from being spoiled by the sun.

Bottles of red wine were stacked side-by-side on the last table before the register. Perhaps to add to the sauce. For drinking too, I'm sure. I picked up a basket from the front and started with the tomatoes.

Hands, eyes, smell, I whispered to myself.

First, which ones felt firm, but not too strong. It was no use having to wait a week for a tomato to be ready. *We'll have to grab some more later in the week anyway.* Nonna's words from when I was young ran through my head.

One that doesn't feel like it will go bad by the afternoon. One that would be perfectly ripe tomorrow, or the day after. To use today if you need to, but tomorrow, or later. It can't be too small either. Sofia taught me that.

We've got to feed you and your Papa, so it has to be nice and big. It has to be around the size of mine or Nonna's fist, otherwise it's no use. If it can only fit in your hand, but not ours, it's no good.

Can't be bruised either. *Some of these grocers are dishonest people. They think if they turn it on the good side we won't notice. They want to rip us off.*

The bruised ones are damaged, and the yucky flavours will ruin our spaghetti.

Always check the tomato's back, the bottom and its top. Even a small yellow or green spot can spell trouble. Use your eyes.

Be wary of the sun, Raffaele. They can look perfect at the start of the morning. But the sun can suck all its juices if it's been outside for too long. *That's why we come early, but you still need to be careful. A lot of these merchants travel across Sydney selling their tomatoes, and Saturdays can be the last day before they collect a new batch.* Always look carefully.

Then, smell. Hardest to master, but the most crucial step.

A tomato can be the perfect size and deliciously red, but if it doesn't have an earthy, calm smell that reminds you of Nonna's Bolognese, it's no good.

No smell is also a problem. *It could mean the sun has already wreaked its havoc. If it doesn't smell like anything, it's probably a couple days from being stinky.* A tomato that smells nice, but isn't too overbearing, is perfect. *That should make sure it doesn't go bad for many days. When we're ready to cook.*

Sofia would perch up from her kneeled position, and begin to scan the stall with Nonna and I. *I taught your Mamma this a few years ago, which was handed down to me by my own Mamma. Who was good friends with Nonna.*

On this morning – a decade after being briefed by Nonna and Sofia – I found five tomatoes that fit their criteria. Each unblemished, just smaller than a tennis ball. They fit perfectly in the palm of my hand. With the calm, earthy odour that Nonna loved.

I looked at the cherry tomatoes (*hand, eyes, smell*), then the onions (*light scratch, then smell*), and ignored the chillis. The bottom of my basket disappeared from view, and the container was reaching capacity.

I was urged to buy a bottle of a wine. A 2020 merlot from South Australia. $40, the bright yellow plastic sign read. No chance. I handed him my $50 note and was given a 20 and a couple of gold coins in return.

The queue now stretched some 20 metres. The other grocers, selling fresh fruit and trendy vegetables, were also doing good business. These weren't walk-ins, which slowed down the pace for these merchants. Shoppers had to point to their boutique vegetable, causing frustration and confusion for the fussy Inner West clientele.

I spotted Sofia and Bella at the back of the queue for the stall I had just left. Sofia brought the green plastic bag she'd always take to the markets, and Bella had taken one of the few baskets still available to shoppers that morning. *Raffaele, what are you doing here? Have you bought enough for the sauce already?* I explained to Sofia that I'd got here before opening and had shopped for tomatoes before a queue could form.

I got tomatoes, onions, beef, all the important stuff. Hands, eyes, smell. Like you and Nonna taught me. The ends of her lips creased to a smile. She nodded, then changed the subject. Her and Bella, who was facing away from me, were going to grab some other groceries. *Some more tomatoes and a bottle of wine. Just to be sure.*

***

I cut through the back of the school to get home. I took my basket with me and didn't plan on returning it. It would be my new carry bag. An alternative to being identified as a Clarendon rugby player to any and all passers-by.

This was the school your Pappa and Zio went to, Sofia told me when I was young. *Nonna used to walk the two of them here in the mornings, and collect them in the afternoons. I'll get Zio to dig up the photos for you.*

She told me this 10 years ago. Thankfully, I didn't hold my breath. The school assembly hall could have some old photos hiding somewhere. It was a rectangular room with a high ceiling, polished floorboards and skinny windows overlooking the schoolyard. It was right in front of me. I looked down the corridor, and pushed open its wooden doors.

Leftover gazebos and packing shelves for merchants to borrow were scattered across the front of the hall. Otherwise, it would've been locked. I ducked past the debris to arrive at front of the hall, where a dusty stage rose one metre above the wooden floorboards. It had three stairs leading to the stage, which held the Bunnings chairs reserved for the principal and vice-principal, who would preside over the assembly each week.

A series of square doors under the stage hid the miscellaneous, dusty items nobody cared for anymore. I swallowed my breath, threw off my thongs, and went exploring. The square cabinet leading to the spare gazebos had been peered open that morning. It was my only way in.

I couldn't see anything. I pinched my phone from my pocket to get a light, revealing a deceptively deep chamber. I kept on crawling.

I pushed past a sports bag with eight plush dodgeballs and sports bibs in sun-bleached milk crates, before twisting around old chairs and desks to get to the ancient material at the back.

There were banners for sports teams, trophies the school didn't care to display, and old sports shirts lost over time. I even uncovered a milk-crate containing a batch of Sydney 2000 Olympic polo shirts in one end of the underpassage.

There were a bunch of crates stuffed with big, brown photo albums at the back corner of the underpassage. They were made up of hard pieces of brown paper that might've been white a long time ago but had become grimy after decades of decay.

I flipped through the albums closest to me, but would fling each away when I realised they weren't what I was looking for. Crawling in the darkness made me impatient, paranoid, and fidgety.

Five books looked promising. They were overflowing with pullouts and inserts of different classes, music recitals, and sports meets. Some in black-and-white, others in colour, none with a chronological timeline or coherent pattern. They would've been thrown into the milk crates and slid to the end of the space by a teacher many years ago. Out of sight, out of mind.

I scanned through the first pages of each album until I found one marked '1976-78'. Instead of sporting an ugly brown covering, this one –

surprisingly – was bound by black leather and cleaner than the albums it lived next to.

Perhaps there was a particularly passionate librarian in charge of the album that year. Or some leftover money to spend. I flipped through the pages, which were firm and had gathered very little muck over the last fifty years.

Vincenzo Leonardi (V. Leonardi) sat at the end of his class photo. His knuckles had been planted on top of his knees, and he had an unimpressed look on his face. He stared at the ground at the end of the hall, past the photographer and his 30 classmates. A strand of scruffy hair looped past one of his eyebrows to partially block his right eye from view. Dad looked unsettled; the small boy glancing at the floor, with only one eye visible to the camera. He never talked much about his childhood, or his life before me.

There were others like Dad. Two other boys, scattered across the front row, looked equally uncomfortable. L. Scagnetti (front, second to right) had a few tufts poking out of his buzz cut. He was smiling but had no front teeth to show. His eyes looked bright, but they were staring at the ground.

The more graceful boys were at the back. They stood tall, arms firm to their sides, shoulders puffed out. Composed and relaxed, unlike their shorter classmates. They leaned into the middle, sporting the same dark orange polos handed to me before Mum and I left Leichhardt. The ones in the photo were just in black-and-white.

The teacher, an elderly grey-haired woman, stood patiently at the end of the front row. She was shorter than most of the boys in the back row and was disinterested in feigning a smile for the camera. The album ended with some pictures from Smith Street's Year Six production of *A Midsummer Night's Dream*. It looked more tragic than tragedy.

I twirled back onto my belly and crawled towards the cabinets. I only saw the dust and dirt on me when the light from the hall windows reached the underpassage. I thought it'd be confined to my hands and fingertips, but it had settled all over my body, staining my t-shirt and khaki shorts with dark, unidentifiable matter.

My crawl turned to a glide. Right knee up, left elbow up. Left knee up, right elbow up. On and on, until I could feel sunlight warming my skin. I felt my way past each of the cabinets, reaching until I found the square already latched open.

I slid out, etching my handprints on the back of the cabinets and wooden floorboards. I reached for my basket, which I'd set down on the edge of the stage, just above the unlocked cabinet square. My tomatoes and onions still looked perfect.

The reflection on the glass inset of the wooden assembly doors revealed the state of my face. Dirt, with two holes carved for my eyeballs. You had to look closely to see skin. My arms told a similar story – bits of fluff and muck had attached themselves to my palms and forearms, all the way to my shoulders.

I washed up in the bathroom next to the hall. Before any of the women could shriek.

39

Making Pasta

December 2022

The tomatoes were simmering on top of the onions when Sofia and Bella strolled through the side door. *Ciao, Sofia. Ciao, Bella.* Their baskets were brimming with fruit and veg, the same stuff I'd bought at the markets. Mine was now cooking in the pan, with some spaghetti and penne.

Bella had a bottle of overpriced wine tucked into her basket. I wondered if she would return hers when the next market came along, or if she'd be hoarding hers like me.

Sofia and Nonna would take me to the markets, but never show me how to cook. Mum would be summoned to the kitchen, away from the dining room table or her desk upstairs. *Raffaele, go find your mother.* She'd help them cook. *Then go play,* Nonna would order.

I commandeered the stove as soon as I got home. The nonnas were moving at a snail's pace through the zig-zagging shopping line, so I knew I'd have enough time to start before Sofia and Bella returned. Even with my expedition below the stage.

I hadn't seen Dad or Zio all morning. It became a sweltering day, which I only realised when I was cooking. The dust from the assembly hall stuck to my forearms and started to crack under the sweat dripping from my head. I could feel sweat bubbling on the edges of my hairline, which had dropped to my temples and past my jaw. Wiping the dust with my shirt would cause an endless fit of sneezing.

Dad and Zio would've trotted to the bay in their thongs, matching white singlets and old nylon shorts, for some respite from the heat. I caught Dad wearing some of my Clarendon shorts the other day. *Raffaele, I'm like Blocker Roach!* It was a rare spry moment from him. *Nope, more like Leonardi! RUSTY Leonardi, the one from the castle on top of the river!* He had never called me Rusty before, even in jest.

Sofia wouldn't kick me off the stove if I'd already started cooking. Bella didn't say a word. She dropped her basket on the kitchen counter, which had already been covered with my ingredients for the pasta sauce.

It would've taken too much time to properly unpack them. I removed the tomatoes and onions from the basket and grabbed the cutting board by the drying rack. The rest could wait.

Sofia, I'm having a go at my own sauce. She was in a huff. Sofia had inherited the kitchen from Nonna after she died, so my place there wasn't right. I extended the olive branch. *You're going to love it. Believe me.*

Okay, Raffaele. She spoke with ominous inflexions. *This is your chance.*

We will take the twins to the bay for a swim. Bella looked surprised. *We'll be hungry by the time we get back.*

She turned to the concrete landing, where Gioia and Mia were drawing a hopscotch court with a crayon set they were bought for the holidays. Sofia shoo'd them in.

We're going down to the water girls – get in and put your swimmers on. Andiamo.

40

Vindication

December 2022

I knew the sauce was good the moment I lifted the lid. Bursts of warm, sweet tomatoes rushed from the pan to the kitchen ceiling, then back to my nostrils for a second wave of delight. The onions, cut into crisp, half-inch squares, gave it a mild sourness that brought extra flavour without compromising the sanctity of the tomatoes.

I replaced the lid, now spotted with the tiniest splatters of sauce, and turned the stove to a low simmer. I pulled up my dining chair, threw my heels on the edges of the table, and tried to keep my smugness for when the side gate would latch open.

Thud, pop, push. And scream. Sofia, Bella, Mia and Gioia were home, and in perfect time.

I sprung up and started to serve. I'd boiled the spaghetti they'd bought that morning about ten minutes before I sat at the dining room table, using Sofia's long wooden spoon – the one Nonna took from Sicily with her – to stir each of the noodles until they were perfectly *al dente*. They were dancing in the big silver pot next to the sauce, slowly being cooked by the flames on the stove.

Raffaele! Oh. Pause. *Oh.* Sofia couldn't see it yet, but she could smell it. Her plate was served the moment she put both feet under the dining room table. I gave her no time to rouse on me. *Ask and you shall receive, Zia.*

Bella and the twins, towels draped across their shoulders, waddled in after Sofia. Each plate was topped with a small basil leaf resting on the apex of the spaghetti. I knew this would piss Sofia off. *Used to disguise a boring sauce,* she would always say.

I walked outside once they were all seated. The softness as they chewed was the only sound I could make out, followed by the clink of their forks hitting the ceramic plates minutes later.

Gioia and Mia burst onto the concrete to restart their game of hopscotch. I slid through the opening before the door closed. Sofia stood over the counter, washing the empty plates over the sink. She stopped and turned to me. *Bravo, Raffaele.*

I shot her a faint smile, then went to grab Bella's plate from under her. She was still sitting but had thrown her legs onto the chair by her side and rolled her head towards the ceiling. *Grazie, Raffaele.* I passed her plate to Sofia and started scrubbing the stove.

41

Leichhardt Oval

July 1987

Vincenzo snuck into his first Tigers game when he was 17. He never needed to check when a match was on; the thudding of footsteps outside his house would let him know. He never forgot that sound. The synchronised smacking of canvas shoes and boots sounded like a regiment on parade.

Vincenzo had gotten out of church that morning by feigning illness. Nothing serious, just enough to make his mother concerned. It was flu season, so it wasn't difficult to produce an explanation. They would go for lunch after the service, probably to see Carlo at Bar Italia as well. Nobody would be home until the afternoon.

Vincenzo could hear what was happening outside much better than he could see. His line of vision was limited to the width of the front door, which spanned about half a metre. It showed a never-ending stream of shoes and pants, entering from his right and exiting to the left. He could see the tops of some children, mostly dressed in orange. Their hands reached up past the denim jeans or trousers of their parents by their side.

Vincenzo pulled the front door open. All he could see were hordes of people. Hundreds came from the bay, or from closer to the shops, almost in unison. Impossible to walk home, he thought. No chance of driving down here either.

It was mainly men in their fifties and sixties. They wore black winter coats with jeans or khaki-coloured chinos, dark-coloured shoes with rubber soles, and leather belts to hold their waists in. The bald ones wore old man caps to cover their domes. They would tuck their hands in the front pockets of their coats and glue their arms to their sides to stay warm. The only exposed hands were those clasping a beer can, which would be crushed and thrown to the kerb once erased.

The kids didn't seem to mind the cold. They'd reach their hands into their parents' coats – the kangaroo pouch – to stop them being swallowed by the crowd. The gripping and scratching of their rundown sandshoes on the gravel and bitumen were drowned by each step their fathers would take. Most kids wore shorts and a t-shirt, with a hoodie or oversized knitted jumper on their torso.

Vincenzo counted six women in the crowd, all devoted to child control. They'd lag a couple of paces behind their husbands, who were deep in conversation with similar-looking gentlemen, each gesticulating with their non-drinking hand and only expelling air to howl in laughter.

Vincenzo raised his eyes to scan the ends of the street. When one set of legs turned out at one side, another arrived at the other. The same denims, corduroys, shoes and children.

All with a tinge of orange and black. It was more obvious on the kids, who wore the colours in horizontal stripes, or with a black V over a long-sleeved orange jumper. The scarf, with the same stripe-on-stripe pattern, was more fashionable for older men.

There were some black-and-white scarves spliced in. Younger men, in their twenties or thirties, wore shirts with the white V on a black long-sleeve shirt. They were too young for old man caps. Beanies with a magpie sewn on the front protected their domes from the chill.

Vincenzo pulled the gate at the end of the front landing the width of his side and slipped into the crowd. He would see where they would take him. Vincenzo still planned on beating his family home. If he didn't, he would say he was out looking for them.

Vincenzo's street was one of several inundated by foot traffic. There were some closer to the bay, and others flowing from Norton Street. Vincenzo had to dodge parked cars and street poles to find space to walk. The winter coats and old man caps had multiplied. It must've been a big game.

Tigers vs Western Suburbs on a Sunday afternoon. The movement of the crowds slowed as they approached the oval. Vincenzo looked to the sides of the street, where mountains of crushed beer cans lay. The odd punter flogging spare tickets stood next to the telegraph poles or street corners, their screams only being heard by the handful of men gliding directly by them.

Vincenzo slipped behind a group of middle-aged men, who had formed a five-person front line that no ground staff would penetrate. He stayed on the tail of the man in the middle, a particularly boisterous larrikin with a clean shave and an aversion to any voice but his own.

Blocker's going right up the guts today. Who's going to stop him? They'll be thrown all the way back to Haberfield on the first hit-up.

A couple paces behind the man was his wife, a blonde-haired, short woman with a leather jacket and denim jeans. She'd been carrying her young boy since Vincenzo caught the group 100 metres from the ground. She was keeping to the edge of the road, while the men dodged the parked cars mounted to the footpath.

Not a lick of notice was paid to Vincenzo at the gate. He kept close to the larrikin, staying on his hip as he entered the ground. He jerked to a stop once he got through, causing Vincenzo's torso to bump into the small of his back. He didn't turn and continued his yarn with the bloke next to him.

One of the men that Vincenzo trailed raced to the grandstand by the main entry to greet a familiar face. He was now 20 metres away, but his voice pierced the ends of his eardrums.

Junior's the best backrower in the country, mate. He should be leading the Blues, let alone the Tigers. Terry could use some of that grit. Watch it happen, mate. I'm telling ya.

Vincenzo ditched the group and headed for the hill. The players were retreating down the race for their final preparations.

He had never been to a Tigers match before, but it all felt very familiar. The noise from the ground could be heard from his living room during each match. The only thing he had yet to experience was the actual game.

The Balmain cheerleaders, about a dozen blonde and brunette women in sleeveless, orange-and-black crop tops and miniskirts, sprinted to the centre of the field. They displayed an array of acrobatic feats over a mix of sleazy rock and pop songs.

Vincenzo first heard the catcalls after a spectacular show of synchronised flexibility. The cheerleaders descended into a seated position, before tucking their legs into their chests – toes above their ears – and rolling onto their backs before springing to their feet. They were facing the main grandstand, which is where most of the noise came from.

The crowd was a plethora of middle-aged men and regretful wives. Pockets of younger people stood by the gates at the very top of the hill, perched by the beer stands. The kids, many of Vincenzo's age, hung off their parents like an accessory, happy to be involved but without much of a choice in the matter.

The wogs camped by the corners of the hill. They were in packs sitting on picnic rugs or leaning onto side gates. The fronts of their hands hardly fit into their denim jeans, which weren't protected by their knitted jumpers.

The other wogs were working the game. They thudded up and down the paved stairs, flogging soft drinks, ice-creams, pies and Chiko rolls from containers strapped to their shoulders. They were the same age as Vincenzo. The older ones got the better gigs, pulling pints or showing Anglos to their seats.

It was five minutes until kick-off. The merchants already stunk of beer and melted nougat. But they'd persist. *Like a schooner off the wog boy's back.* They'd thump down each aisle, all the way to the fence, and then back past the wooden plank seats. Shouting until someone flashed a banknote at them.

They winded the hill just before kick-off. They'd look for the closest flight of stairs leading to the grass and walk all the way to the beer stands. Kids would chase them down, with a handful of coins jiggling inside their fists. Then walk back down, and onto the next bay.

Some people were kinder than others. Families would call them over, forking out cash for a Heart or Cornetto, sometimes a Fanta. Some of the blokes were cruel. The ones on the aisle would jolt their drinks to the side just as they were walking past, causing it to splash onto the boy's chest and basket. It made the merchant and their sweets reek.

The Tigers, led by the adored duo of Blocker Roach and Junior Pearce, were running out. The roar from the hill reverberated to the other side of the oval, and back onto the ground. The Magpies supporters had no chance. Even when their team ran out, you could only hear cheers for Balmain.

Junior started the match with a bang. That first tackle. *Oomph*. The hill loved that.

Vincenzo still hadn't found a place to sit. The planks below the hill, and those behind each of the goal posts, were stacked with winter coats and old man caps, each attached to a hand gripping a beer can.

The demountable beer stands hardly got a rest during play. They had the tiniest windows, just big enough to take an order and for a beer to be handed over. The younger blokes by the hill never left their feet.

The merchants were still getting grief. No one wanted to hear their shouts anymore. *Piss off, wog. Can't you see we're trying to watch the game? Come back later.* It didn't stop them from trying. Down. Fence. Up. Hill. They had some sort of quota to meet.

Vincenzo eventually settled on a small knoll perched on a few blades of grass. There was very little growth on the hill, he discovered. From up close, it was more of a dust slope and dried mud, which had developed a texture like concrete. Pouches of grass popped up in random areas, mostly at the bottom, but the rest was eroded by footsteps and beer cans.

A group of wogs were camped in a loose semi-circle a few metres behind Vincenzo. They chewed on focaccia from a clear plastic lunchbox. It was placed in the middle of the men, who'd poke their hands in each time they finished speaking.

They'd shout in English when something exciting happened. *High-tackle! Penalty! Try!!*. Then back to the semi-circle, and Italian.

They were the only ones that didn't get up at half-time. It was hardly acknowledged; those on the edge of the semi-circle turned away from the ground, and they continued chatting. In a literal social circle.

Most of the men headed for the urinals, then after that, the beer stand. They would walk through one door for the urinal, out the other, then find the drinks queue. Lines for the demountable stretched to the concrete concourse, which had become packed with punters moving in every direction.

***

Vincenzo was in the thick of it. He stepped down to the concourse after the half-time whistle, observing the mass exodus towards the bathrooms. He also had to go but didn't want to miss the start of the second half. There were some rules he still didn't understand about the game, but he enjoyed following along.

There was a bush covered in dead, brown leaves on the other side of the fence, which was at the top of another slope leading towards the suburban grounds near the bay. Vincenzo trod up, sidestepped some other children with the same idea, and relieved himself.

This had placed him on the far end of the ground, behind the footy sticks. This was where the diehard Tigers faithful congregated; they wouldn't dare leave their seats over the interval. They'd send their kids or wives out for beers, and only rise from the wooden planks to stretch their bones or celebrate a try.

The cheerleaders, in the same orange-and-black costumes, had returned to the field, performing another routine lapped up by punters around the ground. *Let's Dance* played across the loudspeakers this time. The cheerleaders, lying on their backs, would kick up alternating legs on each of Bowie's *bum, bum, bum*s. They'd jump up, wave their pompoms, and retreat for the next row of dancers to do the same thing. The music echoed through the ground, becoming muffled towards the end of the routine.

Vincenzo headed for the grandstand. It looked to be reserved for those in leather boots and smooth old man caps. They sat in invisible groups; separated by the class or quality of the coat they were wearing.

They'd drink from glasses, poured by waiters in suit pants and waist-coats, and eat from silver platters or paper serviettes. They used a special entry that connected from the street to the back of the grandstand. Like a secret tunnel, to avoid fraternising with the uncivilised.

Vincenzo eventually found a standing position by a food truck perched next to the grandstand. The second half was as bone-clattering as the first. Huge people sprinting at other huge people, doing their best to stop the huge person in front of them. The tacklers would assume a squatting position, preparing for the car crash milliseconds away.

Back and forth, tackle after tackle, until one of the shorter, skinnier blokes got his hands on the ball, and kicked it as far as he could. Then they'd chase after it. Then tackle. And tackle again. And smash. Then kick. And do it again.

The skinny guys would stand around looking busy most of the time. They'd retrieve the ball when it was kicked to their end, then run it back, usually towards the skinniest opponent chasing them. They'd inch up when their team had the ball, and pray that none of the big players would run at them.

They were only of any use when they were close to the try line. They'd pass the ball from side to side, short and long, to find a gap in the opposition's defence. It was the skinny guys' acceleration, agility, and athleticism that made the difference. The glimmer of beauty in a game of bone-clattering brawn.

It was the Tiger's skinny players that had the pizzazz over the Magpie's. They could jump higher, move quicker, and had the creativity unmatched by their black-and-white counterparts.

The full-time siren was met with approving cheers. Comfortable win for the Tigers. The pure-leather boots in the grandstand were whisked away, some in the dying moments of the game. The other ones hopped down the stairs to the concourse, and hurried to the street before they could be smothered by the crowd. The remaining bums-in-seats, the older, bigger men with old man caps on their domes, sat back and nursed their beers.

Vincenzo walked to the corner of the hill he found in the first half. Punters streamed down either side of him, most jumping from the concrete buffer onto the concourse. Each step down from the hill pushed another empty beer can towards the ground. The sheer quantity threatened an overflow from the concrete buffer by the concourse, which had now assumed the function of a dam wall.

Vincenzo left when the final wine glass was set down in the grandstand. Punters were still making their way through the gates, but the ground was practically empty. The mud on the hill had been hidden by beer cans – which were now being collected by the same merchants who were selling soft drinks and ice-cream – and the groundsmen were already on the field to inspect the damage.

Some coats and caps were heading for the bay, but most stayed on the main road. *To the leagues,* Vincenzo heard one man say. The victory coaxed the crowd into a careless wander, only ascending to an actual walk once Vincenzo turned into his street.

The hopeless ones were trying to part the seas. They'd inch up cautiously, putting a toe on their car accelerator, then grind to a halt again. They'd blare their horn. Crawl forward, push forward, stop. *Beeeeeeeeeeeep.*

There were no such problems on Vincenzo's street. It was always parked up, so it was only the foot traffic he had to worry about. The cars rendered the footpath useless anyway, so the road was always fair game. He inched his front gate open and slid through. The road was still packed with winter coats and dark shoes, though fewer and fewer were turning from the oval.

The few who didn't continue to the bay seemed to be using his street to cut past the punters dawdling towards Norton Street, or to find a bus to Rozelle.

Vincenzo walked past the landing, up the steps, and into his house. He slid his shoes off on the doorstep to avoid making any noise. He stood for a moment, listening for any movements. Nobody was home. He fell back onto his mattress and shut his eyes.

***

Cheering on the Tigers at Leichhardt became a passion of Vincenzo's. He'd regularly go to matches as a young adult with friends from his jobsite or football team. This continued when he became a father. Raffaele was an easy companion; he'd watch the game with the steely focus of a coach, and hit his hands together when a try was scored. Vincenzo remembered how his eyes would shimmer when the Tigers ran out to rapturous applause, or when confetti was thrown to celebrate a win.

Vincenzo would always invite Fiona to the games, but she was too busy working. Giovanni wasn't keen either; they'd still use his car from time-to-time to watch a football match, but his sporting interest would stop there.

Vincenzo hadn't been to a match in years, though memories would flood back each time the Tigers played at Leichhardt. The thudding footsteps and noise made it impossible to shut out his past life. He wished he could forget that sound. It didn't seem as loud when he was drinking on the back landing.

42

Deck the Back Landing

December 2022

It was now the week before Christmas. I'd been living in the kitchen the past few weeks, only leaving to buy more tomatoes and onions from the grocer, or to seek temporary shelter from the heat. Or to sleep.

Sofia pushed me into sauce-making duties after I proved myself worthy a couple of weeks back. *Raffaele!*, she screamed from the kitchen one morning. I was still lying in bed, wide awake but yet to concede it.

I meandered down, but nobody was there. Sofia was gone, Bella was off with the twins – the daycare had closed until the new year – and Dad and Zio were working. Or swimming. Or otherwise out.

Four plum tomatoes and two onions were sitting on the countertop. Sofia's green plastic bag lay next to it, empty. She must've gone to the grocers that morning. Nips of oregano were nestled in the fruit basket, and I could see some ground beef, probably just bought from Woolies, taken from the fridge and resting next to the tomatoes.

You weren't so bad on your first try. Sofia's internal dialogue was running through my brain. *Do it again.* I set what I needed on the counter, just next to the stove. Crush. Chop. Sort. Onto the saucepan, stir, simmer. And wait.

It would be served for lunch. My breakfast, anyway. I boiled the spaghetti while the sauce was cooking on low, only taking it off when the pasta was perfectly chewy. I served mine into the high-rounded bowl normally used as a sharing plate.

I dipped my index finger into the sauce and touched it to the side of my gum. Better than last time. The rest of the sauce was served on evenly distributed plates of spaghetti. I kept a couple of spare spoonfuls especially for Gioia and Mia, who'd need a hearty lunch when they returned. For Bella's sake, if nobody else.

Like last time, I didn't wait for or seek their approval. After cleaning the saucepan and pot, and resting it on the drying rack, I grabbed my keys, walked up the hill, and queued at the bus interchange.

I'd grown fond of my bus driver. An older, scraggly fellow with a longwhite beard distracting from the thinning greys up top. He could've been a mall Santa if he wasn't driving buses. He looked away when I forgot my Opal card and would always wish me well when we approached my stop. *Beautiful day mate! Make the most of it.*

Santa would scoop me from Balmain Road, drive through Rozelle, past the main intersection, and spit me out a couple hundred metres past the Balmain shops. Just a small trot to the water, where I'd spend the afternoon in an enclave of Sydney Harbour.

Sometimes I'd bring a book. First, a memoir of some 20th-century communist we would be studying for English next year, but that quickly became dull. I'd then resort to listening to music from my phone. On other days, like this one, I would lie on the boardwalk, inches from the rockpool, and let the sunshine wash over me. I arrived home a few hours later, to an empty countertop and drying dishes.

You've taken my job, Raffaele! I'd never seen Bella so animated. *Onwards and upwards for you and your sauce. The girls love it too. You'll have to do it again. Tomorrow?*

Sofia would take stock of the kitchen at night and plug the gaps the next morning. She'd place the ingredients on the countertop, next to the stove as requested, and let me cook. She didn't wake me up anymore, but it was expected that it'd be done for lunchtime. I think Sofia and Bella were equally relieved to have me help.

Bella would laze around in the afternoons, as she had always wanted. Sofia was tired of her apathy, but she was accustomed to it now.

Dad looked confused the first time he tasted my sauce. It was on one of those weird December days, where after weeks of pure sunshine, the heavens opened across Sydney. For hours at a time, with patches of overcast clouds reminding of the potential for more rain to come.

A day you could perhaps expect in the first week of January, but hardly the middle of December. *Raffaele.* Dad glanced up from the dining table. *This is you?* I paused for a second, then hurriedly nodded in his direction. He didn't know what to say. *Bella, did you help with this? Sofia? You're not making Raffaele buy this with his own money, are you?* He turned back to me, his eyes soft and sincere. *Raffaele, does she owe you any money?*

Sofia explained. She said Bella was helping her pick out the ingredients, even though she never shopped with Sofia anymore. Dad bought it. He gave a slow nod, his shoulders in tune with his head's up-and-down motion. He kept on eating, without any chatter, then rose. He gave me a firm pat on the shoulder with the inside of his palm and made his way to the toilet.

Dad and Zio put up the Christmas tree later that day. It was the only domestic duty they would do, and the one their wives had been bugging them to complete. *Your children are begging for the Christmas tree, Vincenzo. We're only a couple weeks away! Let them enjoy. Per favore.*

The tree was held by two rusted metal poles that clicked into one another. They combined through a small, semi-spherical button on the top beam that locked into the corresponding hole on the bottom beam. It was painted green but had been picked off over the years to now show the reflective silver colouring.

Each pole was lined with plastic, stick-like branches that sprung artificial twigs when pulled from its centre. They stretched to create the illusion of a healthy, puffy Christmas tree. Lush in the corner of our front room, next to the TV. As always, it was placed by the dining table, which was now protected by a silky, unstained white tablecloth. The tree towered over me on my last Christmas here, but it now felt like the small, approachable friend without much to say.

The angel, a tired, worn-out ornament bought decades ago was held by the single plastic twig pointing to the ceiling. It symbolised the birth of Christ and reminded us of the disintegration of the tree. There were only two ornaments that weren't there when I was young. They had tiny handprints on them, and 'Gioia' and 'Mia' printed with a red glitter pen.

The twins rushed to the tree, screaming, when they returned from the shops with Sofia in the afternoon. Seconds later, my legs had been wrapped by each of their arms. Their cheeks were pressed to the bottom of my thighs.

Buon Natale, Raffaele.

Buon Natale, girls.

Christmas in St Ives

December 2022

Fiona said goodbye to her son and hung up the phone. She inhaled until she could feel her lungs reach the sides of her chest and exhaled until her shoulders crouched over her torso.

It was the morning of Christmas Eve, and the first time Fiona had heard Rusty's voice since he left for his father's home weeks ago. They had messaged most days when he first moved to Leichhardt, but their texts had become far less frequent in the lead-up to Christmas.

Vincenzo texted Fiona twice. First when Rusty arrived at his home, and second to ask her permission for Rusty to stay over the entire summer. Rusty's father had no warning of his son's arrival at his home, but he was overjoyed to have him. He conveyed this to Fiona, worried she may think Rusty had been a burden on his wife Bella and their two young children. Fiona didn't mind; she was happy Rusty was happy. Vincenzo's delight was a bonus. Though they hardly spoke anymore, she harboured no ill-feeling towards her ex-husband.

Christmas snuck up on Fiona. She had spent her days and nights crouched over her desk in the weeks since Rusty left, inspecting each of her client's six-month reports and projected outlooks for the rest of the financial year. December was always a crunch time for Premium Accounting Solutions – they'd hire two casual bookkeepers to manage the load. They were especially stretched this year, when two of her full-time accountants took annual leave in the fortnight leading to Christmas Day.

It was a blessing in disguise for Fiona. Piles of documents and stationery sprawled across the table in the backroom of her St Ives townhouse. It was one of the few pieces of furniture that Phil hadn't taken away. She'd annotate, highlight, circle and dogear pages from the binders dedicated to each client, which became smudged by coffee stains as the weeks wore on. The copies in her Crows Nest office, where she'd spent most of her days, were much cleaner. These were the documents she would show to her clients.

The work wasn't over by Christmas Eve. Fiona still had a mountain to climb, one which would be achieved by another week of early mornings and late nights behind her desk. But she needed to call her son. She planned a nice Christmas Day with Rusty, which she hoped would make up for the turbulence he had to endure over the last month. A Christmas ham from the butcher on Mona Vale Road had been put aside for Fiona, who made her order on one of her rare shopping outings a few days prior. She thought she and Rusty could spend the afternoon on a gentle walking trail on the edges of the national park, burning off some of the calories they put on at lunch. Rusty sounded enthusiastic over the phone. It made Fiona smile.

***

Fiona could feel the nerves gurgling at the bottom of her stomach when she arrived outside Vincenzo's home on Christmas Day. She had buried most of her memories of Leichhardt, including her distaste for the long, narrow road leading to the Leonardi household. To her relief, there was a parking space next to the front landing where she used to take down the washing in the mornings. Fiona mounted the kerb with the tyres on her left side, and pinged Rusty.

Fiona was anxious about seeing her son again. For all the issues Fiona faced with Vincenzo's family, she couldn't fault their stability. They each had a role, which they executed with unerring dependability. It was what made Fiona an outcast in this home. She prayed it wouldn't sweep Rusty away from her.

Rusty emerged on the landing and was walking towards her. She leaned across the console to hug her son, before squirming the car out of that cursed street.

Her nervousness manifested in a series of overzealous questions about her son's life in Leichhardt. She asked how he spent his days, about Vincenzo and his children, and living with Sofia and his Uncle Giovanni. Rusty was a tad overcome by the questions but was obliging in his answers. Fiona feared questions from her son about her own welfare. She never gave Rusty a chance to ask them.

Concerns of a confrontation spurred Fiona to fast-track the day's proceedings. Fiona was panicking, and she felt helpless against herself. She hadn't seen her son for weeks, and she was actively minimising the time they would spend together.

Fiona didn't know why she did this. She hated how often she felt out of control when it came to her actions around other people. Especially the ones she loved so deeply.

The Christmas ham, with a generous helping of salad and a sour-dough loaf, was served while the morning Christmas mass was still in session. Neither Fiona nor Rusty was hungry, and neither had many points left to share after their small talk in the car. Fiona was hesitant to talk about Vincenzo and his new family, and Rusty didn't want to talk about Phil.

Fiona's agitation had exhausted her. She excused herself to put on her sandshoes after their de facto brunch, but found herself face down in bed instead. The appeal of an afternoon walk had lost its shine for Fiona, who started to think Rusty would prefer to be back by the water in Leichhardt anyway. She jolted up after catching herself asleep and returned to find her son on the lone couch in the backroom of her townhouse, next to the modest stash of Christmas presents.

Fiona was self-conscious about her gift for Rusty. Two cans of deodorant, and a packet of socks and underwear from Rivers. Her son never asked his mother for anything, making him an easy-going boy, but extremely difficult to buy gifts for.

Rusty looked pleased when he peeled off the blue wrapping paper, fixed with an image of Santa nursing a beer can and cigarette between his fingers. She was embarrassed when she opened Rusty's gift for her; a white tablecloth with an embroidered zig-zag pattern and tiny circles, a few millimetres in radius, spotted across the linen.

It was a beautiful gift. Fiona was in awe of her son. She smiled and reached for Rusty so they could embrace. The tablecloth was slid out of its plastic sleeve, and thrown over the dining table, which still held the remnants of their Christmas lunch. The bumps where the ham and salad bowl were couldn't detract from the beauty of Rusty's gesture. He was a beautiful boy.

Fiona's body went stiff again. Rusty wouldn't want to spend the afternoon with her mother, in boring old St Ives. She wasn't sure if she wanted to be there either. Rusty was led to his mother's car less than 20 minutes after they opened presents, right around lunchtime. Fiona offered the remains of the Christmas ham to Rusty, which he politely declined. There was never any shortage of food in his father's house.

Fiona and Rusty spent the journey to Leichhardt in a comfortable silence. Neither wished to blemish their limited time together with topics they didn't wish to speak about. They had a lovely day, if a short one. They could both cherish that.

Fiona turned down Norton Street and inched her car to the Leonardi house. Two identical, navy-blue towels were drying over the railing on the front landing. Fiona knew these belonged to Vincenzo and Giovanni – they had been swimming in the bay together since they were children. This was no different on Christmas Day, when they'd skip morning mass for a dip before the foreshore got overrun.

Fiona turned to Rusty, who was already facing his mother. She hugged her son and planted a kiss on his cheek. Rusty unclicked his seatbelt, and with his measly Christmas gift under his wing, shuffled past the front gate, onto the landing and into the house. He turned back before shutting the front door to wave at his mother, who hadn't moved an inch since her son rose from the passenger seat.

With that, Rusty disappeared behind the front gate, and into obscurity. Fiona expelled the tension left in her lungs and dismounted the kerb. She headed back to her part of the world.

Christmas Day

December 2022

Christmas Day started with a splutter of tiny footsteps and squealing. Gioia and Mia, down the circular staircase, belching their excitement through their untuned vocal cords.

We had huddled together for church the night before. *Where me and your mother got married*, Dad whispered as we sat at our pew. Loud enough for me to hear, but impossible for anyone else to make out.

Bella was adorned in her Sunday best. It was a Saturday, as it goes. She led us to the congregation, which was already forming at the front of the church. Sofia, the one insisting we all go, strolled in alongside Zio, leaving Dad and I trailing at the end.

It's tradition. Sofia was lecturing me from the kitchen counter earlier that night. *You'll do it, and you'll enjoy it. We can then open presents tomorrow.*

***

I'd just returned home when Sofia gave me my orders. Less than an hour before, I was drifting in the Balmain baths, focusing on my breath and losing staring contests with the sun.

George Gregan's autobiography had been living at the bottom of the plastic container I stole from the markets for most of the summer. I stashed it behind a bedside drawer I never used, and only brought it out when I went swimming.

This guy wasn't the tallest or the strongest, but became the Wallabies most capped player. A bloke who wasn't even born here, and raised in the Canberra suburbs. Branderson had run over from the other side of the quadrangle on the last day of school to hand the book to me. *This is what will bring your mentality to the next level.* Personal copy, apparently.

I didn't think Branderson would hang around for the last day. No teams were training, and the gym was closed. I was certain he was coming to lambast me for something I did wrong during camp week.

I hadn't touched the book all summer. It was initially hidden in the bottom of my Clarendon bag, which I only rediscovered after unpacking when I arrived at Dad's. Hardback, so still in decent nick. Small creases on a couple of pages, one with a miniscule tear, but hopefully Branderson wouldn't notice.

But in case he did, I ought to have something to say about it. Some commentary on the Brumbies' favourite son would go a long way to allaying any hill sprints I'd be given for damaging his precious book.

It went from the bottom of my school bag to the bottom of my shopping basket. Protected by my towel, which gave a soft landing to my $2 sunglasses and hat. I got off the bus around midday – after enough tomatoes and beef to feed Sicily had been turned into sauce – and had splashed around before opening the hardback.

I read the first few chapters. *My upbringing, The schoolyears, Rugby, Rugby, and More Rugby.* Then I skimmed the pictures. The paper was thin, and the book was two inches thick. All I needed was a talking point from some excerpt with redeeming qualities. I learnt that from English.

It had some of Branderson's personal annotations, scribbled in the margins with a blue ballpoint marker, under a chapter called 'Climbing Everest: 1999'. He talked about motivation, hard work, and grit. The metaphor used by Gregan sounded familiar.

Rusty, you got to outwork your opposite number. Do you think the wingers at Saint Marys are taking weekends off? What about the boys in the junior A teams? They're chasing you down. And if you slack off, they're going to get you. Branderson had been plagiarising George Gregan this entire time. It made me laugh.

I closed the book and decided to enjoy the day. The baths were sparse today; I suspect many regulars had family plans or were away for the Christmas weekend. It was just me, head down on a thin, crumbling cotton towel separating my body from the plank below. I was there until I lost the sun over the peninsula. I strolled up the hill and hailed down Santa Claus.

Then came the shock of the day. Dad, in a collared shirt. It was short-sleeved and yellow, with thin white lines running down it. And Zio. In an orange polo, khaki shorts, and enclosed shoes. Sofia's arm was directing me to my bedroom, where a hanger holding a light blue dress shirt and denim jeans was resting on the doorknob. We were due for the evening service.

***

Back to Christmas Day. Bella was chasing the twins precisely ten seconds after they laid eyes on the presents under the Christmas tree. The thudding of her footsteps down the corridor put me on edge.

She trod down the staircase and quieted the girls with an almighty *shush* that could be heard from anywhere in the house. I came down ten minutes later. I didn't see the point of holding up the proceedings any longer, especially while the girls continued to snicker and laugh downstairs. Sofia, in a thinly veiled summer gown, tiptoed after me. Zio and Dad fronted up ten minutes later.

I don't think they knew how to treat me. There were adults here, and there were children. No awkward in-betweens. Certainly not ones who showed up on their doorstep at the start of the month and were only meant to be around for a week.

Zio and Sofia handed me an envelope with a card holding $200. Four fifties, by my count. Dad and Bella bought me a brand new, cream-coloured lamp, wrapped in last week's La Fiamma.

Back when I picked you up from school, Dad explained to me. *Your teacher told me you might be moving into a nicer room. If the rower doesn't. The lamp can help you study late at night.*

The ends of his lips made the smallest crease, which turned into a nod. You're welcome, it read.

Bella rose from her dining table chair to hold me. One hand around my back, and the other cupping the back of my head.

Gioia and Mia were already on the back pavers, racing their identical red-and-blue tricycles against each other. They rolled from the top, near the Bunnings chairs, all the way to the bottom, steering away from the steel fence that narrowed as the hill went on. Gioia sped through – hardly slowing – relegating Mia to second place on the makeshift raceway.

The fridge was stuffed with containers of Bolognese. I had the day off. I climbed the staircase, envelope tucked under my arm, and the neck of the lamp, shaped like a square bracket, trapped in my fist.

I set the lamp on a spare paper folder to keep it from being dirtied by the dust on the carpet. Then I fell onto my bed and stuffed my face in the crevasse between my pillows.

I wondered what would happen for the rest of the day, now that the formalities were over. Sofia and Bella would probably take the twins to church again, but I don't think Dad or Zio would tag along. Maybe they'd make a dash for the bay. The sun was already piercing through the windows, creating a harsh glare on the metal poles of the Christmas tree. It wouldn't be long until the entire foreshore was swamped by light-patterned gazebos and huge umbrellas.

Mum

December 2022

um would be picking me up at 10am to spend Christmas Day to-
gether. *Just you and me. We'll have lunch, open presents, maybe go for a walk through the park in the afternoon.* Our plans only materialised on the morning of Christmas Eve. I had barely heard from her since I left St Ives. *It'll be great.*

Her enthusiasm on the phone wasn't replicated at the kerb. It started when my phone pinged. 'Out front!'. I couldn't blame her for not wanting to come in, or show her face. I called out from the front step, and stepped into Mum's car before I could hear a reply.

She whisked us onto Balmain Road, and we crossed the Parramatta River five minutes after I stepped in the car. There were no more than a dozen joggers or walkers on the bay when we crossed over, and only a handful of cars on the roads. Everyone was still at home, opening their presents.

Mum seemed spry. *How's the past few weeks been? Has it been manic with the little kids around? What about Dad. Is he holding up okay?* It reminded me of when Phil drove me home in the early years of high school. He was thoughtful in his questions, but always kept it surface level.

You've been lapping up all the recent sunshine? Mum's fourth question in a minute. *Down by the baths? Nice. Your Dad and I went down there back in the day. I wonder if they'd installed new planks by now, some of them had nails and spikes pointing out from all places when I was last there.* She drew for breath. *That was a long time ago now.*

Each of my responses triggered one of her flashbacks, none of which were riveting. I feigned interest in her long-winded responses, giggled at the punchlines, and asked the leading question each time she wanted it.

We were back in St Ives half an hour later. It was much busier than Leichhardt.

Families dressed in light-coloured sundresses and short-sleeved button-ups filled the streets leading to church. 10:30. It made sense. The families on the other side of the road, across from the church, walked in packs to the traffic lights. Like the crowds for the Tigers matches Dad used to take me to. This seemed much more orderly though.

Mum turned right at the big intersection, past the families on the footpath, before accelerating down each long, straight road until we were on our own one.

The huge trees, which hung over the cars and trailers on the kerb, were in perfect growth during high summer. The electrical wires snaked through each of the trees, popping out of one just to hide away at the next. They were hardly visible between branches, which had become overgrown while the council workers were on holiday. The street was otherwise identical. Nothing drastic happens in just a few weeks.

There wasn't a Christmas tree at home this year. The few presents Mum bought were bundled onto the lone couch in the living room.

Light-blue wrapping paper, with a design of Santa holding a beer can and cigarette, preserved the mystery of each gift. They were pinched on the ends without a millimetre of slack on any corner. Wrapped flawlessly.

I put Mum's present at the end of the pile. It was a white, linen tablecloth I had spotted at an antiques shop in Balmain a couple weeks ago. On the day Santa wasn't driving, when I was dropped in the town centre. It had a striped pattern on the outside, which made a zig-zag with a thick, embroidered line just inside the edge of the tablecloth. Tiny holes, half a centimetre in diameter, lay at the centre of the squares formed by each zig-zag.

Mum glanced at the gift for a moment, surprised by it. Perhaps it was the newspaper clippings I had over it. The shop folded it into an A4 sleeve hardly thicker than paper, then handed it to me. There was more old newspaper in Dad's house than there was wrapping paper. She held the wrapped present in her hands for a moment, curious as to what it was, then returned it to the couch and walked back to the kitchen.

Tucked in at eye-level – the mantel of the whole fridge – was the Christmas ham. From the St Ives butcher, cut in half for us. Phil glazed it with a special brush, but this one hadn't been touched. *You ready to eat, Rusty?* Mum had grabbed the ham, which was sitting on a small plastic platter in the fridge and slid it onto the counter. A sourdough loaf and butter were already on the counter. Mum must've put it out before she collected me.

I wasn't ready to eat. It wasn't even 11. I hadn't had breakfast, and yet it still felt a bit premature for Christmas lunch. We hadn't opened our presents yet. Her eagerness surprised me. *Yes Mum. Ready when you are.* She pierced her lips and let out a smile. The first slice of ham was cut three minutes later.

Neither of us were hungry. Mum kept on slicing the ham, cut-by-cut, into pieces no thicker than a few centimetres. Until the pig sprawled to all sides of the platter, like an oversized belly with rolls of fat hanging just above the table. Six cuts were slapped onto my plate. A nice, ceramic one that Mum would bring out for special occasions. She put two slices onto hers, doused it with some gravy, then obsessed over the salad.

Iceberg lettuce, cherry tomatoes, and balsamic vinegar. Contained in the plastic bowl with the green vine wrapped across it. The design had scrubbed off in the wash, so the vine had faded into a collection of different shoots and leaves. The salad covered two-thirds of the bowl, near to where the vine had been completely washed out.

Mum dumped four spoonfuls onto my plate and showered it with balsamic. My plate was almost invisible. She pinched a few tomatoes and a strand of lettuce, then paired it with the slices she'd put on her ceramic. We both ate passively, politely, while Christmas lunch ran its course.

There was a lot not to talk about. Mum didn't want to hear about my life with Dad, and neither of us wanted to talk about Phil.

Gone in two weeks or less, he was. The place was the same as I left it earlier that month. All his stuff, the useful things, was gone. We had one couch, occupied by presents, next to the dining table, which now had three chairs instead of six. The smooth, wooden TV stand remained, but didn't have anything to proclaim. Phil took the TV a week after he left. Mum had moved a frame – our fake Jackson Pollock splatter – onto the stand.

Lunch was over by 11:30. Mum said she was going upstairs to put on shoes for an afternoon walk but didn't return in any hurry. She was lying face-down in bed when I checked on her. The doona cover was wrapped over the top of her head, and her toes hung over the mattress, just a few inches from the ground. I kept the bedroom door at a slight crack, and crept downstairs. Without making a sound. Mum came back down in her slippers 20 minutes after I found her.

Sorry, Rusty! Must've dozed off. Shall we open presents now?

I was gifted socks, underwear, and Lynx Africa. Like the everyman. No complaints: I didn't ask for anything else. Mum was surprised by the tablecloth. My gifts used to piggyback from Dad or Phil. I had never had to put too much thought into a gift for her before. She spread the tablecloth in her hands and traced the zig-zag with her index finger, only straying to roll her fingernail over the tiny, stitched circles.

I saw her smile. *I love it.* She got up from the couch, which we were sitting on either end of, and threw the tablecloth over the dining table. There were little bumps where the salad bowl and plates were, but she didn't care. *Thank you.* She drew a breath. *I love it.*

We lurched around the couch for a little longer after that. I got up and snuck my hand under the tablecloth to grab two extra slices of ham. It was cut so thin that most didn't even touch the tablecloth, which I thought could blemish the food. Only now – at lunchtime – was I ready to eat.

I suppose you'd want to spend the rest of the day with your father. Mum hadn't spoken since unwrapping her present. Her eyes refused to meet mine. I looked to the ground and shrugged. Mum stood up and reached for her keys.

Back to Mona Vale Road. The congregation was gone; perhaps they'd be back for an afternoon or evening service. The shops were empty, but the roads weren't. Families travelling from one commitment to the next. Mum seemed withdrawn.

Over the Parramatta River. Just next to Clarendon. Perhaps that's where Branderson was spending the day. I hoped he wasn't. He never spoke about a life outside of rugby. I didn't know who he would call family.

Mum's head gently rolled to her left as we crossed the Gladesville Bridge. From one angle, you could see the Harbour Bridge from here. The sun was beginning to fall from the middle of the sky. It was shimmer-

ing on the water, which was dancing back at the sun in a show of gratitude.

Mum's gaze shifted away from the water, and onto the foreground.
Her eyes caught mine, and we smiled again.

46

What is a Child Without Parents?

December 2022

Vincenzo didn't think Fiona would say hello. Their interactions had been sparse since she left him. Only to arrange sleepovers for Raffaele, or to let him know of anything happening at school. He was sad to hear about her separation from Phil, but equally shocked that she called him to share the news.

Raffaele retreated to his bedroom shortly after they had opened presents on Christmas morning. Bella had been onto Vincenzo for weeks about Raffaele's present. She was stumped and wanted her husband to take the lead. They thought about giving him cash, but Bella wanted something more thoughtful. She dragged Vincenzo to Big W the previous weekend to pick something for his son. They settled on a plastic, cream-painted lamp; Vincenzo thought he might need it for his new room. Bella approved, and with that, it was thrown into their shopping trolley.

Vincenzo loved having Raffaele at home during the summer. He wished he didn't have to spend his days working, and wasn't so set on wasting away on the back landing. He didn't know why he sabotaged himself like this.

He was taken aback at how independent Raffaele was. He knew teenagers as lazy, apathetic and hostile to parental figures. That was Giovanni's boys. Vincenzo's son was proactive, intelligent, and had the right balance of cheek and charisma. Bella wasn't always Raffaele's biggest fan, but he didn't expect this. He was surprised to learn that Raffaele had been entrusted with preparing the pasta sauce, and even more shocked when he tasted it. Raffaele used to accompany Sofia and his Nonna to the Saturday markets when he lived here. Vincenzo wondered if he remembered this. The idea that he might touched him.

Raffaele was due to see his mother on Christmas Day, but Vincenzo didn't know when. He rose from the back landing, where he was watching his youngest children play on their tricycles, to see his eldest. He hoped Raffaele would have enough time to come to the bay with him. It would be one of the first times they'd spent time together since he had been back here.

Raffaele's room was empty. Only his shopping basket, stuffed with swimmers, a towel, hat and book were left. His mother must have already picked him up. Vincenzo was sure Raffaele said goodbye, he just couldn't have heard it over Mia and Gioia's playful screams.

Vincenzo slumped onto Raffaele's bed. He had tucked Giovanni and Sofia's Christmas card and enclosed cash into one of his pillowcases. $200. Vincenzo thought this was a very generous gift. He knew he'd hear about it from Bella later that day.

He lay flat on the bed for some time, thinking about the future. He prayed that Raffaele would be successful in his final years at school, and hoped Gioia and Mia would be happy too. He didn't have any doubts about his future. He'd be working, then sleeping. Work, then sleep. Back and forth, until his back gave out.

Vincenzo rose out of bed. He wasn't sure how he felt about that anymore. Seeing how much of an adult Raffaele was made him realise that he was never allowed to be young. A child can only exist when their parents let them be one. Vincenzo didn't want the same for his other children.

47

First Week of School

January 2023

Slam. Thud. Sizzle. Bang. Summer was over and this was my alarm. Sofia downstairs, cooking scrambled eggs on toast. Then came the shouting. *Raffaele! Up.* She was banging the spare pan on the side of the stove. It was insufferable. *Time to get up!.*

Mum had already written a note excusing my late return to the boarding house. This only ever happened for the country boys, if they couldn't find a ride into Sydney before the school year began. But even that was frowned upon.

It's good to get settled before we get into the swing of things. Patterson would say the same thing at the start of every school year. *New rooms, new faces, you don't want to be dealing with that while balancing your sport and studies.* It was framed as instructive but enforced like law.

The note informed Patterson that I, due to a series of personal circumstances that won't be divulged, would be unable to get back to the House before the first day of school. I sincerely apologised for the inconvenience, and hoped this wouldn't be too much trouble. Regards, Fiona (on behalf of Rusty Leonardi).

My delaying tactics were only fleeting. I spent the previous night reassuring Sofia of my safe passage to school the following morning. I'd walk to Balmain Road, jump on the first bus to Rozelle, then one up Victoria Road, and then hop off outside the sandstone castle. Sofia traced the route on her thick yellow Gregory's directory, maintaining a keen focus with every flip of the page.

***

Her sons Leonardo and Luca came back once that summer. Christmas Day, after lunch. *To miss the theatrics*, Luca teased. They came with a box of cannoli and a case of Peroni Reds. A peace offering.

Sofia jostled the door open when she heard the gate unlatch and met her two sons in an almighty embrace on the front landing. Zio wrestled out of his Bunnings chair on the back pavers after hearing the commotion. He'd been sitting here with Dad since Mum dropped me back.

Zio took the beers from Leonardo's grasp, and dropped the cannoli on the kitchen counter. They met their father at the bottom of the staircase, which they winded with a sense of relegation. Zio bumped his torso against each of them, reaching over and completing the hug with one solid thud on the tops of their backs. The twins were still mucking around outside, and Bella was hiding upstairs.

Raffaele? Leonardo was speaking to me in a soft tone. He had dark features and combed, slicked-back hair flowing to the collar of his navy-blue polo. He showed me a grin. *It's been forever. How you been?* I rose from the kitchen table, where I'd been sitting since I returned from St Ives. I thought about making some pasta sauce, just to make myself useful, but felt too full to do anything but laze around.

We didn't kiss, hug, shake hands or fist bump. I nodded my head at Leonardo, then turned towards Luca and did the same. I didn't recognise them, but said I had a faint recollection. I could hardly believe we shared a room together. They spent most of the afternoon being peppered by Sofia with questions about what they were doing with their lives. I engaged in the most passive way possible. Encouraging smiles, nods to show I understood, and eye contact when they glanced my way.

***

Other than those few hours on Christmas Day, Sofia had been taking Bella from job to job all summer or keeping the place running herself. While I took care of the cooking. This week, it was all about getting me ready for school. This morning, getting me fed before school. Breakfast was always a free-for-all, and never involved pots or pans.

Today was different. There were no plans for me to be back in a while, especially on a weekday. Sofia made me set out my school uniform on a coat hanger last night, which was resting on my doorknob. I had taken most of the stuff I needed for school from Mum's on Christmas Day.

A few button-ups, shorts, socks, and the school tie. I took the blazer too, even though it wasn't part of the summer uniform. My rugby shirt and pants were already with me; I was using them when I went to the gym over summer.

I shuttered down the spinning staircase in my pyjamas. A dash of pepper had been splashed on my eggs, which had been placed on two pieces of toast at my place on the table. I could hear Gioia and Mia racing around upstairs. Daycare wouldn't open for a few more hours. They had gone back last week, to Bella's relief. Sofia sat down beside me. Then she issued my marching orders.

Go upstairs once you finish eating and get changed. I'll walk you to the bus. You remember what we said last night? Get the first bus to Rozelle, then the next to school. It won't be a long trip, so it doesn't matter if you can't find a seat. It's important to be organised before your classes start.

Sofia lost her appetite three blocks into the walk. Less conversation, more staring at the ground. She looked surprised to see me in my school uniform. A short-sleeve, button-up shirt, khaki pants and grey school socks, pulled to the top of my calves. With a blue-and-green tie that hung half an inch below my undone top button.

It was a harsh contrast to my summer attire. Even the button-up I wore to church on Christmas Eve. Sofia snapped a photo of me on the bottom step of the front landing, just as she once did with her boys. And what I'm sure she'll do three years from now – along with Bella – when Gioia and Mia start at Smith Street.

Sofia turned back home the second she could see Balmain Road. A sardine tin had just pulled in to collect a hoard of commuters, which prompted Sofia to give me a final squeeze on my wrist and turn for home. I flashed Santa Claus a smile as I hopped onto the bus, and with that, I was flung out of Leichhardt.

48

Drawing Circles

January 2023

A squeeze on the neck and a slap on my ears. That's how Patrick welcomed me back to Fairfax House.

Oi, Rusty. About time you got back.

He had been here since Saturday. *Wanted the room at the top of the house, but Patto reckons that belongs to you. Lucky he's in love with you.* Patrick was already heading to class.

Patterson was predictably bubbly. *Rusty! How are you, mate? Come with me, I got something good for you.* He led me to the top of the staircase, and to the very end of the corridor.

The rowing team tanked over the holidays, so they had no hope for nationals. The room was mine. That smug rower Alistair wouldn't be getting the satisfaction. Beyond that, I didn't care too much.

The place, for all its maintenance over summer, looked the same. Some tiles were cleaner, and there were less leaves in the gutter. Otherwise, same miserable place.

I didn't have a TV, but thought a mini-fridge could fit in the corner of my room. The TV stand could be used as a counter. To keep easy-make meals, like noodles and ramen, cooked from the kettle I'd inherited from last year's house captain.

I missed the start-of-school formalities, like the House welcome and icebreaker. It gave me an easy out from being a Year 7 mentor, which no senior student wanted to take on. It still felt like a matter of time until Patterson would ask me to look after an unfortunate young soul.

The rest of Clarendon hadn't changed. The gardens were perfectly cut, the boarding house equally disciplined and unruly, and the teachers overly serious.

You are all now the leaders of Clarendon. This was the party line the new Year 11s would be asked to toe. *It's time to step-up, both in the class-room and the school community. This one's the dress rehearsal for next year.*

I couldn't sleep on my first night back. The country boys had met for a smoke in my old room, directly below me. They must've thought I didn't know about it, despite my subtle clues last year. I didn't know who the room belonged to now.

It wasn't the muffled giggles, the smoke traces, or even the smell keep-ing me up. I was ready and willing to fall asleep, but my body wouldn't comply.

I could slip into unconsciousness most nights, exhausted by a full plate of classes and training during the day. Rugby sessions were on hold for the first couple of weeks, to give the rowing squad full access to the gym. All the coaches were focused on the rowers. I'd even seen Brander-son taking them through hill sprints.

My body turned on its side, and my eyes peered open. The quadrangle was deserted. The only signs of life were the puffs of smoke, rising and disintegrating at the bottom of my window.

Click, click. They were lighting another doob. I turned towards the corridor and planted my feet on the floor. I opened my door ever so slightly, and crisscrossed down each flight of stairs, touching each step with the ends of my toes to avoid making a sound.

Silence fell on my old room when I glanced by. I made three small, soft thuds towards the room, just for the fun of it. The lights had never been turned on – they weren't stupid – but I could imagine the panicked gestures and gesticulations they'd be making to each other.

The room's occupier would look fast asleep if a teacher were to peer the door open. With an occasional snore or grunt to sell the rustling sounds that first aroused suspicion. The rest would hide under the bed or in the closets, praying for the outside noise to dissipate. The doobs would be put out on the windowsill and flicked onto the quadrangle. One of them would creep down before roll call the next morning to dispose of them before a teacher made the discovery.

I turned away from the room, and continued tiptoeing down the staircase. The ground floor, where the teachers slept, was dead quiet. I wondered how they felt about being back at school. It did mean they could stop pestering their parents or friends for their couch and have something more stable again. But this place was never a real home. I slipped out of the House and headed for the school gates.

The view from the science classrooms was liberating. Not one cloud over the water, which was shimmering under a full moon. I shuffled to the end of the small, concrete platform overlooking Sydney Harbour, sitting down and crossing my legs once I reached it.

I inched myself forward, letting my feet dangle between the gaps in the steel fencing. Looking out as far as my eyes could see.

My brain only allowed me to tiptoe here, even though the school was empty. The janitor didn't lock the staircase anymore. Nobody would be coming to get me.

There was not a dash of wind on the harbour or past the heads. It gave a sense of calm. Summer holidays were over, but the sun was still out, and the days were still long. The foreshores were packed, and the beaches were booming. We looked so glamorous in the daytime.

My eyes moved from the skyscrapers in the west, Parramatta I suspected, past the bay near Leichhardt, and to the Sydney skyline. A few other buildings peaked over the north shore peninsulas, tracing a tangled line from Milsons Point to Clarendon. All the way back to me. Returning for another year.

One foot dangled forward, then the other. Like a swing set thrusting away, only to end up right back where it started.

Epilogue

November 2024

Rusty, or Raffaele, eventually found his place inside the sandstone castle.

Despite Branderson and Patterson's fierce protestations, he dropped out of the rugby program four weeks after the summer break. He didn't want any special attention from his teachers, and was sick of Branderson and his mind games. His coach had been especially tough on him in his first weeks back at school, even threatening to have him suspended after discovering a tear on one page of his George Gregan autobiography.

Raffaele didn't give Branderson any reason or notice about his decision. It only came to light after he stopped attending his after-school gym sessions.

He had a new fascination. History. Studying the past to understand the present. Twentieth-century Australia became his specialty. Stolen Generations, Gallipoli, Harold Holt, Bob Hawke, and the Republic referendum. He developed a particular interest in post-WWII European migration, and its impact on the modern Australian identity.

Academic essays and books piled up on the TV stand in Raffaele's room. Topics included the influence of migration on Australian cuisine and identity, the treatment of diaspora communities in urban centres, and the intersection of migrant cultures with white Australia's 'beach-and-bush' lifestyle.

Raffaele's new passion inspired him to try other pursuits. After studying the work of Banjo Patterson, he decided to give poetry a go. He mainly wrote free verse, inspired by his observations of the world around him. He would share his poems with his English teacher, who encouraged him to submit his work to the school's weekly paper, the Clarendon Chronicle. He was first published in Year 12, with a poem called 'An Ode to Home'.

Wasting his sporting talents made him an unpopular figure in the boarding house. It was rumoured he only used rugby to get the dorm on the top floor, and that he never cared about the team or the school crest in the first place.

Patterson couldn't name him house captain at the end of Year 11. His hand was forced. It was given to the rower Alistair, whose boat finished seventh at nationals that year. Patrick, who'd made a surprising push into second grade rugby as an overzealous flanker, was made vice-captain.

Raffaele finished top of Modern History at Clarendon, and accepted an early offer from the Australian National University to study a Bachelor of Arts, majoring in History.

But Raffaele didn't want to go straight from one classroom to another. He wanted to try his hand in the real world first. He found a job as a deckhand on the Tyrrhenian Sea, which would keep him busy during the European summer. He planned on renting a car and travelling the Italian coastline beforehand, starting in Palermo and ending in Genoa.

***

Phil moved into his apartment in the city the day he left Fiona. He had intended to sell the place, as he had discussed with Rusty's Mum, but never got around to doing so. He negatively geared it while living in St Ives, and was considering getting tenants in to add a new income stream.

He kept doing the odd consulting job for a mate, or a friend of a friend. He didn't tell any of his colleagues about his impending divorce, but it wasn't hard to hide. Nobody asked him about his personal life.

Simon and John, his two friends from school, didn't care for him either. Phil caught up with them in the weeks after he left Fiona, but they never asked him about himself. They yarned about work, the footy, and the money they'd lost betting on the footy. Or complained about their own relationship woes.

The first time Phil was asked about his marriage was at Christmas. It was Barry, asking him where Fiona was. Phil was at his father's doorstep for Christmas lunch. He paused, then told him they had separated. Barry grunted, then returned to the fridge to fetch another beer.

***

Fiona spent the summer giving her life to her clients busy over Christmas. She was otherwise face-down in bed, in the same position Rusty found her on Christmas Day.

Fiona had tried to make Christmas as normal as possible but knew her son would see right through her. But, as always, he was too polite to say anything.

Things got better for Fiona in the new year. She threw herself into different hobbies, including joining a local pottery class. Which she found insufferable. It made her realise she had outgrown St Ives.

Leaving wasn't much of a chore. She sold her townhouse to a wealthy family with a six-year-old daughter starting at an accelerator school on the other side of Mona Vale Road. She bought a two-bedroom terrace home in Annandale with her share of the sale. Phil got some, but not as much as Fiona, as was negotiated in their divorce settlement. Fiona's new place wasn't far from where she grew up.

***

Vincenzo and Bella continued raising their children. Vincenzo supported Gioia and Mia through any job that popped up, and Bella, with the help of Sofia, kept on chasing after them.

To Gioia and Mia's distress, Raffaele wasn't around nearly as much as he was during the summer. Of course, this was largely due to school. His Mum's home in Annandale became his default base outside Clarendon, though its proximity to Leichhardt made it much easier for him to meet Sofia and Bella at the markets on a Saturday morning, or for Sunday lunches at the old dining table.

Raffaele was still asked to make his famous pasta sauce for the house. He'd pick out the ingredients at the markets on Saturday, then come back to cook. Just like in summer. He'd plate some for lunch and put the rest in Tupperware containers stacked in the freezer. He rarely stuck around to see it used.

Gioia and Mia were getting ready to start at Smith Street. The same orange-and-blue uniforms used by Sofia's children over a decade ago had already been prepared for them. Mia had developed an interest in painting, and had started hanging her pieces, usually a splash of bright colours on a canvas pad in no obvious pattern, in random places across the house. She'd even sticky-taped a few in Raffaele's old room. Gioia preferred playing outside. She'd take her *Pappa* to the football fields by the bay on Saturday mornings, insisting that he play goalkeeper while she kicked balls at him. Vincenzo loved every second of it.

***

Sofia grew tired of watching over children in that house. She'd been doing it for the last 20 years, and felt as if she had done her service.

Along with her husband Giovanni, they made a deal with Vincenzo and Bella: once the twins started school, the house would belong to them. They'd buy a place using the money saved by living without a mortgage for most of their adult lives. A one-storey detached home in Haberfield, walking distance from the cafes on Ramsay Street, was what they were looking for. It would let them move on, and allow Vincenzo and Bella to raise their children without two empty nesters lingering around them.

Giovanni continued to work with Vincenzo, but did so less frequently and for shorter hours. Sofia would start her weekends at the markets on Smith Street, and spend the morning cooking with Bella and spoiling her *nipoti*.

Her boys Leonardo and Luca would stay in the spare bedroom when they wanted to sleep over. They would rarely do this, but never complained about the sleeping conditions when they did. More often, they'd meet their parents – along with the rest of the Leonardi family – in Leichhardt for Sunday lunch.

Raffaele was also a regular in Leichhardt for Sunday lunch. He'd make a special effort to be there on the weekends when he couldn't get to the Saturday markets or cook pasta sauce for his family.

***

Raffaele caught the bus to Smith Street on the first Saturday after his last exam of Year 12. He had been waiting for an entire week for the Modern History paper, which came last in a four-week exam period. His room in the boarding house was already packed up, and most of the other Year 12s – who were already finished with exams – had left.

Raffaele left Clarendon for good after the exam, which he knew he aced. His two duffle bags, filled with clothes, toiletries and his desk lamp, were lugged to the bottom of the staircase, where Patterson was chatting with Fiona, who parked her car right outside the House. Patterson, with a flickering glimmer in his eyes, shook Raffaele's hand and gave him a hard pat on the back. He wasn't sure if he would ever see his star student again.

Raffaele tapped off the bus at the Leichhardt interchange, two blocks from Smith Street. It was 20 minutes to eight. He had arranged to meet Sofia and Bella on the hour, outside the school gates. He turned away from Smith Street and walked towards the water.

Despite it almost being summer, it was a cool, windy morning. The oak trees by the bay ruffled in all directions, while the unkempt plants and tall grass by the foreshore jolted with the erratic rhythm of the water. Joggers wore nylon hoodies and didn't dream of taking their shirts off.

The weather didn't worry Gioia. Raffaele could see her from afar, standing on the penalty spot with a football at her feet and her father between the goalposts. She would trap the ball with the bottom of her sandshoes, take four steps backwards, and punt the ball at Vincenzo, who had covered his coffee mug behind one of the goalposts.

Gioia abandoned the game once she saw Raffaele walking towards the field. She sprinted to him, jumping up for his torso and wrapping both her arms around his body. Raffaele caught his sister, propped her up on his side, and carried her back to the field.

Vincenzo gave his son a nod, and rolled the ball back out to the penalty spot. He had no chance of saving any of his Raffaele's shots. They were hit with power, and placed in whichever corner of the goal he pleased. He had better luck with Gioia, who could only kick the ball a metre either side of him. Vincenzo didn't think it'd be too long until his daughter would also need a better goalkeeper.

The ball was rolled back to the penalty spot and controlled by Raffaele with the toes on his right foot. He flicked the ball up to just above his knees, caressing it with a touch on each of his thighs before passing it to Gioia. She flicked it back up to Raffaele, who wrapped his right foot behind the ball, still floating in the air, and zipped it past Vincenzo, into the top left corner of the goal.

Gioia squealed. It was an involuntary reaction. She'd never seen a better goal scored in her life. Her scream drew a self-conscious laugh from Raffaele, who turned away from her sister to face the foreshore.

Vincenzo turned away from the field to fetch the football. It had been lodged beneath one of the oak trees, next to some shrubbery planted to decorate a newly installed playground. He winched the ball from the garden and walked back to the goalposts.

Raffaele and Gioia weren't at the penalty spot when Vincenzo returned. He lifted his eyes, and steadied on the goals at the other end, closer to the foreshore. Gioia, arms flailing and legs in overdrive, was being chased by Raffaele across the field and towards the water. Raffaele grabbed Gioia by the hips when he caught her, lifting her into the air and onto his shoulders. Gioia then placed her hands over Raffaele's eyes, blindfolding him and sending her into a fit of laughter.

Vincenzo placed the football behind one of the goalposts and picked up his coffee mug. He looked forward. Raffaele had taken Gioia off his shoulders, and was twisting her body through the air, like a spaceship dodging an asteroid attack.

Vincenzo leaned on the side of the goal post, took a sip of his coffee, and smiled. His children were at play. He basked in the sweetness of it all.

About the author

Daniel Lo Surdo has written about Sydney's major affairs and cultural events since he was a teenager. This includes as a reporter for The Sydney Morning Herald, and as editor of City Hub Sydney, the Inner West Independent and Bondi View. He has previously written for The Daily Aus, Australia's fastest-growing youth news media service, and the Star Observer, Australia's longest-running publication for the lesbian, gay, bisexual, transgender and intersex communities.

Growing up in Sydney is his debut novel.

He can be contacted at www.daniellosurdo.com.